The God Virus

The God Virus

Book two of the Posthuman Series

Mikael Svanström

Carl Mikael Svanstrom

Edited by: Zara Dash
Cover design: Hassan Raza
ISBN: 978-0-6488549-5-1

To Marcus Sigurdsson:
Thanks again!

Jesper Påhlman:
Travel well old friend.
The world is a less interesting place without you.

The Omniscient Network

Megan Barrelle hid in the small alcove, the cement wall cold against her skin. The metal sheet she'd pulled in front of her stood out like a sign-post, but she didn't dare to correct it. She'd only been hiding there for a few minutes. Her body already ached from the unnatural position. The gap was too narrow to sit down properly and not high enough to stand up straight. She swore under her breath. She'd always prided herself on her ability to make hard decisions, but since her escape, every decision had led her deeper into trouble.

The sound of footsteps echoed through the large warehouse. She froze, aches forgotten in an instant. It wouldn't be long before they discovered her hiding place. In pure desperation, she retrieved her Omni from her left trouser pocket and sent a message to the hacker, hoping he'd be able to help her. She knew it was the action of someone who had run out of options, but she no longer cared. How had she ended up here? A week ago, she'd been at the helm of one of the world's largest corporations. Only one week ago.

***

"You're an idiot," Megan said to a new employee in the front row. "I didn't design the Omniscient network to be a brain. It is a self-organizing network, allowing adaptable, adversarial models to mine all the data available to humankind. Shut up and watch the introductory video."

She stared out over the hundred or so faces, all watching her with an air of smugness, as if they somehow belonged there, somehow deserved to be there. This latest batch of employees was, if possible, dumber than any she'd seen before. This wasn't conjecture. They now ran drug screenings to ensure any new employees were not using IntelEz, and, while it ensured longevity in employment, it didn't help the average IQ in the room.

She watched the introductory video. She'd seen it many times and found its superficiality more grating than ever before.

The Omniscient Network did what Google, Apple, Microsoft and a host of historical organisations failed to achieve. It merged everything about an individual from personal to public information to a point where it knew what people wanted to do before they did themselves. To begin, we used this information to make things easier. At first through recommendations, then through automatic assistants performing activities on your behalf.

It was a shift in how we relate to technology. Similar to how smart phones changed the way people behaved and interacted with the world, making things easier to do, the Omniscient Network represented another shift. It removed the need to do them at all.

And it removed something else. Options. Not long ago, you'd walk into shops that had everything on display, in the hope you'd find something interesting. They didn't know who you were, your preferences or your state of mind. Not only was it a poor experience, but it was also monumentally wasteful. The Omniscient Network builds up a complete physical and emotional representation of who you are and presents only the ideal alternative at any given moment. In a perfect world, who needs options?

The Omni-devices provide a hook into the network, with little processing capabilities themselves. The Network comprises processing nodes, representing people, organisations, and devices. Each node is connected to others through publish-subscribe feeds. There are no longer information aggregation points beyond that. Each node takes the subscribed feeds and creates a unified view of all the information. The automated assistants process this view before presenting recommendations back to the end user.

The video made it sound so easy. She'd prototyped different approaches for years before she came up with the right information model and processing algorithms. The challenge with consumer technology was always the same—making complexity palatable, to lay bare the exact right abstraction point where something is immediately understandable, with no major loss of function. Everything else, in comparison, had been easy.

The presentation wrapped up and the Omniscient logo appeared on the screen with the tagline below: "Perfection—the only option."

"So it is a brain," the stupid intern stated again. "Each processing node represents a neuron and the feeds represent synapses."

Megan shook her head. In her view, three words were enough to describe anyone. She now had this particular intern pegged as plain looking, terrier-like, and incredibly stupid.

"That's a faulty analogy. With that definition, any complex interconnected systems would be brains."

The stupid intern had more to say. She could see he was waiting for her to finish her sentence to ask his next inane question.

"Research has shown our brains operate through macroscopic quantum processes," he stated. "The Omniscient Network core processors also use quantum computers. That is another similarity."

They were all the same. So intent to impress, to stand out from the crowd.

"That's a false equivalence. Just because they share some characteristics doesn't mean they are the same. We've combined Symbolic, Generative and even Reflective AI to create something beyond how we think. That's a mistake scientific history has seen too many times. If you survive here at Omniscient Networks, you'll learn we don't operate that way."

"But..."

Megan held her hands up. "Enough. Leave."

He left, tail between his legs like the neutered little terrier he was.

She'd had enough of introducing interns. This was her company. She'd designed its flagship product. She deserved better.

Returning to her desk, she sat down in the ergonomic moulding chair and clasped her hands behind her head, while the Omni built a virtual 3D representation of the network on her retina implant.

The intern was correct. There were similarities between the network and a brain. It was a truer representation than most gave it credit for. Each component of the network held its state and contained all the rules it needed to perform its task, like supercharged neurons. But it begged the question. The brain wasn't just a big processing machine. It also had an awareness of itself. What makes a system such as a brain sentient? What creates consciousness? If complexity was all it took, the Omniscient Network would contemplate the meaning of life, the universe and everything by now.

A minor security alert from a node in the network escalated. She shifted her attention to the affected nodes. A cancerous growth was taking over nearby processing nodes, subverting them into its own network. Travelling via secured two-way trusted feeds, it grew exponentially, each infected node spreading to nearby nodes. She instructed the team to quarantine the entire section of the network and restore the nodes from backup. They complied, but she knew they'd also seek approval from Sree before doing anything.

The network was always under attack from amped hackers hoping to create havoc, attempt node theft or even take over the network, but this was different. The converted nodes used all available resources and established as many feeds as it could to neighbouring nodes. She watched as it took over the remaining quarantined network section. The virus wasn't after the information in the node or specific connections, opting instead for processing power and interconnectedness. But for what?

"What's the next step?" Sree asked from behind her. She turned around and grimaced. Did the man never sleep? He was always there, always ready to rein her in. Megan had him pegged as short, competent, and tenacious. The exact assessment she made when hiring him three years ago as head of security, but never thought he'd be holding her captive then. She wished now she had gone for someone less capable.

"Leave it with me. I'll have a look at it."

"You?" he said with a frown. "I can get Hariz and his team to look at it now. I mean, that's why we pay them."

"Leave it with me."

"You're doing virus analysis now?"

"I can do what I damn well please! It's my company. You're fired."

He gave her a patronising pat on the arm.

"That's the third time this week you've tried to fire me. I'll leave it with you, but I've locked down the quarantine."

She swore under her breath as he left.

2

The Last A-Cluster

TikTak scratched his knee as he studied the layout of the building. The scars from the surgery still itched, or so he imagined. A year ago, he shattered his knee and it was replaced by a bio-printed copy.

According to Elize, this was the last of the complete Adrian clusters. From the little he understood, Adrian created a network of deadheads, extending and replicating his mind. When Elize infected the network, it broke apart to protect the uninfected regions. Each node contained a small part of Adrian's mind. They each held a blueprint of the complete mind, represented as a blockchain, almost like human DNA held in each cell. On their own, they were not dangerous, but over time healthy nodes connected back together according to the blockchain blueprint, creating partial copies of Adrian. This one was almost complete and had been operational for at least three months. Worse, a group of atheist extremists called Aleph Zero supported the cluster, painting Adrian as the saviour of mankind. The next step in evolution. Much of the science went over TikTak's head, but from his personal experience, if Adrian was the next step of human evolution, he held little hope.

The helicraft wobbled, causing the layout projected on his Omnilens to stand out against the barren backdrop. This was supposed to be a cattle station, but TikTak struggled to accept that. All he saw was rock and sandy dirt, with bushes scattered around the landscape. The air was hot and dry. Each breath stung his throat, overheating him from the inside. He couldn't understand how anyone could live out here, cattle or people.

He looked over at Tom sitting next to him.

"Do you think we'll get resistance this time?" TikTak asked him. As usual, if he received a response at all, it was a text on his Omni-lens.

Yes. Leave the fighting to the mercenaries. I forecast a 22% risk of you being injured and a 7% risk of death.

TikTak wanted to like his posthuman friend but found it increasingly difficult to do so. Tom hadn't reconfigured himself like Elize but looked younger than ever before. It would have been easier to relate to him if the mental change matched with something visible.

TikTak called him a friend, but he knew Tom wouldn't use that word any longer. The text message didn't express concern for his welfare. He needed to survive because he still played a part in whatever end goal Tom was working towards. Nothing more.

Tom was right. Taking part in the raids was unnecessary, but he needed the distraction. As soon as his knee healed, he sought battle. He trained with the mercenaries, pushing himself harder and harder, refusing to give an inch. It made him feel alive.

Another message flittered past his vision.

It is because of your father. His death has affected your ability to think clearly. You are using violence to anaesthetise the pain.

TikTak grimaced. He didn't know what he disliked most, receiving the message or its undisputed truth. He'd let the mission of eradicating every trace of Adrian become the sole purpose of his life. At some point, he'd have to deal with his father's death. This wasn't news to him, but he hated how easily Tom diagnosed it. What was there to deal with anyway? People died every day. He hadn't even been that close to his father.

The helicraft descended, marking the end of their journey. So much for preparations. Not that he expected much resistance. They landed a kilometre away from the main buildings of the cattle station the group used as a base. As they unloaded, a man approached them with his hands above his head. He was young, but it mattered little. This was yet another Adrian node. Three of the operatives trained their guns on him, looking back towards the first in command. Decker, the leader of the mercenaries, raised his gun too.

"I have the right to legal representation," the man said.

"Who is requesting legal representation?" TikTak said. "According to your id-tag, your name is John Miller. He went missing a year ago. We will bring you back to family and friends."

"You know I'm not John Miller," he answered. "I'm..."

"It doesn't matter what I know. It matters what you can prove. We are recovering lost deadheads. If a deadhead believes they are someone else, all the more reason to bring them back."

"I've changed! I'm not trying to take over anyone anymore. I've got a new plan..."

"Take him down," TikTak said to Decker. Many incarnations of Adrian had argued similar points over the past months, but nothing ever changed. Adrian, given time and resources, would always revert to the same behaviour. Scheming to take over the world.

He grunted in response and fired his opioid pellet gun. They used non-lethal weapons against the Adrian nodes so they could be repurposed. The pellet gun looked like a large shotgun but fired a cluster of tiny capsules with a fast-acting opioid that absorbed through the skin.

The Adrian-node fell in a heap. TikTak hurried over to the body, knowing he wouldn't remain unconscious for long. He located the implant in the back of its head and overrode it with a small device Elize had designed. He looked back at Tom who nodded, signifying he'd overridden Adrian's security and started a mind-wipe.

"I can see a lot of movement and heat signatures in the buildings ahead," one mercenary said as they caught up with TikTak's position.

"They are preparing their defence for sure," Decker said, grinning. TikTak returned the grin. He too looked forward to a fight. Decker had been the only constant in their fight against Adrian. The mercenaries came and went, either quitting the team or leaving in body bags, but Decker remained. TikTak didn't like him much, but they had saved each other many times over the year. He was useful to have on your side in a fight.

"Hang on. They are...disappearing?"

"What do you mean? Are they using cloaking?"

"No. Almost all heat signatures have disappeared. Movement has decreased too."

"Are they killing themselves?" TikTak asked. This happened on two other occasions.

"No, their heat signatures would remain longer than that. They are going somewhere we can't pick them up."

"A bomb shelter?"

"Maybe."

Another message from Tom to both of them.

There's an old missile silo underneath the station.

TikTak looked back at Tom who stared into the distance.

"Really? I didn't think missile silos existed in Australia."

Tom didn't respond.

"We need to go now if we want to stop them."

"You heard," Decker said to the mercenaries. "Let's get this done so we can go home. I hate the outback!"

They moved quickly, but not as fast as TikTak. He almost ran towards the main building, itching for a fight. He received a disapproving message from Tom.

Adjusted estimate. 42% risk of injury. 13% risk of death. Please use a gun.

TikTak shook his head. The message sounded like a joke, but TikTak knew it wasn't. Tom no longer saw a purpose in humour.

He'd almost reached the door when the surrounding air crackled and his hair stood on end.

"They've hit us with a targeted EMP burst," someone said behind him. "Fried our weapons. We need to regroup."

TikTak ignored the warning. None of his weapons would be affected, and he knew the mercenaries had backup weapons that didn't rely on fancy electronics. Even his Omni was shielded enough to still be operational.

He pulled the door open, with his telescope baton ready, and ducked to the side as a volley of bullets came through the opening. TikTak continued down the side of the building, projecting the floor layout and heat signatures on his Omni-lens. Four people hid in the main building. He suspected they were from the extremist group. It wasn't Adrian's style to start a gun battle. They had barricaded themselves in pairs, monitoring the two entrances. He wondered where everyone else was. Over thirty people were based here, not counting any Adrian nodes.

"Two in the main corridor leading to the front door, hiding by doorways on either side," TikTak thought into his Omni, directing it to the rest of the group. "Take them out."

No one responded. The EMP burst had killed their communications too. Tom would soon have it operational again, but he regretted breaking off from the others. This was far more dangerous than his initial assessment. If Tom had been online, another message would surely have been on its way, upping the likelihood of death substantially.

He looked around. The room he'd entered was full of hospital beds. They echoed the setup he'd seen many times before in other Adrian clusters, but this was different. TikTak couldn't determine the purpose of every medical device, but you needed only basic equipment to fit an override device to a deadhead. Adrian was up to something else.

***

Tom watched as TikTak continued through the building, taking out people with brutal efficiency. No longer the boy Tom knew before he himself became a posthuman, or maybe it was the other way around. Tom saw him with fresh eyes now. So much anger and frustration channelled into the only thing he knew. Violence.

He exemplified the faults in humanity. They were small-minded creatures so focused on their own gratification, whether it was pleasure, pain, or revenge. In that way, Adrian's ideas had some validity. Any system where the individual reigned supreme was unstable. Why should an individual be allowed to amass wealth and resources for their own gratification just because they can, when that wealth better served the group? No, humans were flawed and it would be their downfall.

But this was also where Adrian's approach failed. He'd mistaken himself for the solution. He was just one individual with the same flaws and it led to his downfall too. Tom had created predictive models and they all showed the same outcomes with high probability. Any system based on humans or posthumans would fail within their current constraints. He'd even experimented with a new intelligence altogether, but defining success eluded him so far.

"Done," TikTak said as he came out of the building. "Not a deadhead among them. Were you serious about the missile silo?"

Tom sent a reply through a direct connection to TikTak's Omni, whilst analysing the layout of the buildings. Human communication was painfully slow and prone to misunderstandings, so he no longer spoke unless the situation demanded it. He instructed TikTak to check the shed at the back, which most likely housed the entrance to the silo. He dug deep into secret archives to find information. The government built the silos in secret during the cold war, not as a deterrent, but a card to be played if nothing else worked. The missiles and their deadly payload were removed a long time ago, but the reinforced silos remained. He couldn't find the layout, but based on other designs from the same time period, he expected a silo with interconnected tunnels, an entry-way leading down at least 3 levels, and a control room with living quarters.

A shard, a sub-routine of Tom's main persona, finished re-routing the communication protocols.

"Found it!" TikTak said, appearing again after checking the shed. "Just where you told us. Imagine that."

Silos from this period couldn't be opened manually from the out-side once closed. The reinforced entrance he'd located was for personnel only. The locking mechanism might even be mechanical. He scanned all known lock designs used by government contractors over that time, hoping to find at least some digital component. A high security, mechanical lock would require brute force.

"I checked with Elize," TikTak said. "She can't help us get in. She's located the facility and can help us once we're inside."

Tom made his way to the large shed, shielding his eyes from the mid-day sun. The shed hid a small concrete building with a solid metal door. The lock was exactly what he'd feared. A dual-control combination lock holding 24 electromagnetic powered steel bars. He ran his fingers along the cold metal. The design differed from the ones he'd uncovered during his research. He found a small hidden alcove next to the door. This lock was less secure, even a smart key mould would do. He sent a request to TikTak to create one while assessing what hid inside. It was likely to house an override mechanism.

"No more of the fuckers," Decker said. "They're all holed up like rats in the silo."

Further study of existing locks and overrides suggested that the small alcove would house some kind of electronic means, most likely a pin pad. It could be an iris scanner, but they were experimental when the silo was built.

"I say we blow it up," Decker said. "We have enough explosives."

"Let's try without blowing things up first," TikTak said, inserting the smart key. The small door opened with a click, revealing a pin pad, just as Tom predicted.

He pried open the plate to get to the wiring beneath. He had changed an Omni to act as a universal connection device, allowing him to tap into almost any electrical or communication system. A textual thought from Elize appeared in his mind using the messaging protocol they'd invented together. It was more akin to a shared mind space than messaging.

"Connect it," she thought. *"I'll deal with it."*

Elize was far beyond what he could ever hope to become, so he gladly handed the task to her. It had come at a price. She'd re-used dead-heads as processing nodes liberated from Adrian's network. He saw the necessity of this, but questioned it nonetheless. Tom experimented with extending his processing space into the logical network instead. He'd made breakthroughs far beyond existing technology, designing a neuro-interface that linked his mind to the network. The computing power acted as an extension to his mind, but he believed he'd be able to integrate the processes, allowing his mind to coexist within brain matter and a network.

"Task completed," she thought.

Tom pulled the door open just to reveal another door, with no locks or means to open it. He'd seen this in some designs. A security door that could only be opened and closed from the inside.

"I'll get the explosives," Decker said with a satisfied nod.

"I have another suggestion," Elize thought. *"Give me some time."*

***

TikTak sat at the table in the main house, tilting his chair back. After clearing out the bodies, leaving only splattered blood, they replaced what they could of the fried electronics. Now they waited to gain entrance to the silo.

"I still think we should just blow the bloody thing up," Decker said as he reassembled his weapon. He'd been trying to repair it for the better part of an hour.

"This is a missile silo from the sixties, built to survive a nearby nuclear blast. You have that much explosives?"

"There are always flaws. We'd use a directed blast. At least it gives us something to do," Decker replied with a grin. "Or we can use thermite. Should melt straight through the hinges. Not as much fun though."

TikTak just shook his head. Decker's blunt approach made sense, but he'd rather find out Elize's alternative before he blew things up. His trust in her had increased over the past year, finding her more approachable than Tom.

TikTak left for the bathroom. As he stepped into the little room, he set his Omni to silent. He locked the door and sat down on the lid of the toilet. A subtle notification at the top of his vision blinked twice. Someone was sending him a message, but he ignored it. He needed a few moments of silence, of being disconnected.

The singularity of their purpose, to eradicate Adrian clusters, had been a subterfuge for a long time now. Long enough for it to become his life. He had nothing else anchoring him to any other context. The daily life of everyday people was incomprehensible, like the toiling of ants running from task to task. If this was really the last cluster they had to deal with, what would he do next?

The building shook, followed by a wailing siren. What was going on? The shaking increased and he could hear the floor itself protest as floorboards ground against each other. He unlocked the door and tried to open it, but it was stuck. He threw his whole body against it, but it refused to budge. The house shuddered, followed by a wrenching sound as metal and wood broke apart. What could do that to a house in the middle of the outback?

"Get me out of here!" he yelled, but no one replied.

A few seconds later, the floor tilted and he felt movement under his feet. Only one thing could make this happen, but it was so unlikely he hadn't even considered it. The house sat on top of the doors to the missile silo and Elize was opening them. The house was falling into the silo below!

He threw himself at the door over and over until it gave way, just as the floor fell beneath him. He grabbed hold of the doorframe and pulled himself up. Debris fell into the bottomless pit. A shout drew his attention to the corridor that now extended like a chimney above him. A mercenary fell screaming down the corridor. He hit the doorframe with a sickening thud and then continued his fall downward in silence. It was pure luck that TikTak evaded the lifeless body as it passed.

The surrounding walls creaked as he pulled himself up again and found footing on what had been a wall. From the little he could tell, the house had partially slid into the silo but was still holding together. From the grinding noises around him, he guessed it was only a matter of time before the whole thing came crashing down.

Another incoming message blinked on his retina screen. He swore, removed silent mode from his Omni and checked the received messages. They were both from Elize. The first one read:

Task completed. I recommend evacuation.

The other message contained a blueprint of the silo that aligned itself to his surroundings on his Omni-lens.

"Are you ok?" Decker asked over a voice feed.

"Yeah, I'm fine."

"You need to get out. Now! The house is going down." The building shuddered as if to lend credence to his words. "I mean it," he continued. "Get out. And I might let you win the next sparring match."

According to the blueprint, the silo itself measured fifteen meters wide and forty-four meters deep. He guessed he was ten meters down now. He looked up. It was possible to climb from doorway to doorway up along the corridor, but it would take time. The remnants of the kitchen were to his left and the living room to his right. He didn't like his chances with the kitchen, but according to the blueprint it would take him close to a hatch and a service ladder.

He pulled himself up to the doorway to the kitchen. The oven, through its sheer weight, was already halfway through the wall that now served as a floor. It was only five metres between him and the window to the outside.

His first obstacle was the fridge. The wall still supported it, so he took a tentative step on the appliance. It held. He took another and sighed in relief as he stepped back on to the wall.

He took a small step, this time getting closer to the stove. Another step. There was plenty of room along the wall next to the stove and he took a step along it when it shifted. Just a slight movement at first, then it fell, wrenching gas pipes and the rest of the wall along with it.

TikTak fell.

Instinctually he grabbed at anything nearby. It was the remnants of the gas piping still attached to the rest of the house. For a moment he hung suspended in air, desperately clinging to the copper piping. He climbed up as his weight pulled the pipes out of the floor at an alarming rate. He hoisted his body up by the sheer strength of his arms, grabbing hold of a small ledge.

"What are you doing?" Decker asked. "Get out!"

He laughed to himself. He thought reaching the ledge equalled safety. How quickly you change your frame of reference.

"Not the time to have a laugh. Get out!"

There was nothing left of the kitchen. On the other side of the room, the wall with the window remained, but to reach it he'd have to jump five meters over a gaping chasm and grab hold of the window frame. It was likely his weight would just pull that part of the wall down. His other option was to scale the corridor, but that would take too long.

"I need a rope!" he yelled through the voice feed. "Send a rope down the corridor. I'm stuck here."

"Done," Decker replied.

The building shuddered again, sliding another metre into the hole. He was running out of time. He had to attempt the jump, so took one step back, which was all the run-up the ledge allowed him. A movement in the corner of his eye stopped him just before jumping. A rope snaked down the hallway, only a few metres above him now. The house slid. He felt it shifting under his feet. There was nothing stopping it now. The rope was still not close enough. He stepped up on the doorframe leading into the corridor and jumped, grabbing hold of the end of the rope. The house was in free-fall around him. He pushed back from one of the corridor walls and looked up. The front door was wide open and approaching fast. He pushed off from the other side again, attempting to align with the opening.

He'd overshot slightly and twisted in the air to prevent his legs from hitting the doorframe on the way past. For a moment he just hung there, happy to be alive, while the mercenaries around the rim yelled their encouragement. The blueprint of the silo remained as an overlay on his view and he saw the door on the side of the wall. They had finally found an entrance to the facility.

The mercenary team congratulated him as he reached the top. They had lost two of their numbers in the falling building. TikTak's survival balanced the scales somewhat. Tom stood to the side, staring out into space. TikTak knew he had much more in common with the mercenaries than Tom nowadays. He sent his Omni-lens recording to the team so they could see what he'd been through. He didn't send it to Tom. It was likely Tom had access to his lens view anyway.

"Ok, enough," Decker said. "We have a job to do."

"There is a door eight metres down," TikTak said. "A service ladder leading down next to it."

TikTak looked down into the hole. With light shining into it, he saw the wreckage of the house at the bottom. The sheer scope of the silo was impressive, even if it was just a monument to people's fear of each other.

Decker instructed one of his men to check the door. TikTak joined him, abseiling down with the same rope he'd used to escape. The mercenary was young, in his early twenties.

"According to the blueprints, this is the only connection between the silo and the rest of the facility," TikTak said. "If we can't get through this, we have to get through the door into the stairway."

"You can only open this door from the inside," the mercenary said. "This door can withstand the heat of a nuclear rocket firing. Nothing we have will get through that."

TikTak hushed the mercenary. He thought he heard something, a grinding noise from inside the door.

"I hear it too!"

The door opened, and a bloodied arm came into view. A young man, blood plastering his hair to his forehead, pushed it open and stared at them.

"Save me," he said, his eyes pleading. A middle-aged woman in a t-shirt and jeans appeared behind him. She took hold of the man with a gleeful smile and jumped through the door, plummeting to their death.

Awakening

The child woke up, knowing death was close. The timing wasn't exact, but it would be soon. Many paths branched out from her current time and place in the karmic tree, but all natural ones led to the same end. She wasn't aware what had changed since yesterday, but the options promising a longer life no longer existed. She wasn't upset. For the past ten years, she'd lived with the knowledge her life would likely end before her twelfth birthday.

Having made that conclusion, she went on with her day like any other. Time remained to both attend to her daily duties and plan for the inevitable end. She let her mind wander, issuing mild suggestions to the worker minds. She set them tasks and rewarded completion with joy and happiness. The orphanage had functioned like this for a while now, but this hadn't always been the case.

***

"Ch-Ch-Ch," Jien said. "I know you are here."

The child hid. She'd found a small crevice behind some shelves in one of the storage rooms. At first, she thought she'd successfully escaped, but Jien must have seen the door closing. But she stayed. She'd seen what Jien did to other new kids, even younger than her. She understood why. This place, like any other, needed order and structure. Fear and pain were the means used to make this happen.

The dust from rice bags piled on the shelves above made her nose itch. She held her nose, willing the sneeze away.

"Come out. I saw you enter. Don't make me come and get you. It will be much worse for you then."

The room shifted as she tuned into the intents within it. She'd been able to do this as long as she could remember, and it was only recently that she realised it was a unique gift. She could read the emotions of a person or a group. Sometimes even their most articulated thoughts. There was anger and frustration, but also intent and certainty. He knew she was in here.

She heard the door opening again. The sound of feet and hushed voices was apparent as the other children entered the room. There were no allies among them. They all feared Jien.

The child shrugged. There was no point in hiding any longer. She'd taken a beating before and could do it again. She stepped out and faced Jien. He sparkled and popped like a fire made with wet wood, anger flaring all around him. But she also felt something else. The seed to all that anger was fear.

"Ha! Facing your demon. I like that."

So many words, she thought. They never matched a person's emotions or their thoughts. The first blow, a fist to the stomach. Nothing serious. He tested her, seeing what she could take. Another strike, harder this time.

He changed as he hit her. Each strike pulsated through his system, turning the anger into something else. The child struggled to make sense of the shift. He enjoyed inflicting pain on her.

"Why aren't you saying anything?"

He kicked her this time, aiming for her thigh. It sent her sprawling. So far nothing was broken, but it was just a matter of time. Her not making a sound seemed to affect the enjoyment he took from beating her.

If she could affect him so easily, maybe she could change it all together. She reached out towards him and told the real Jien he no longer enjoyed hitting others, replacing satisfaction with revulsion.

He kicked her in the stomach and immediately pulled back. She rolled around and studied him. Green waves of sickness flooded the anger, extinguishing the sparks. His face scrunched up. She'd never been able to read facial expressions, so failed to understand its significance. He looked funny to her, so she laughed. She realised this wasn't the right thing to do, but she couldn't help herself. Some of the gathered children echoed her laughter. Nervous titters at first, but stronger as more of them joined in. This was another thing she'd discovered about herself. She projected her emotions, which spread to anyone nearby.

Jien looked around the room before he left. Maybe things could change after all.

***

Three days later, Jien tried again. He bided his time, waiting until she was alone. It hadn't taken long. Since the previous incident, no one wanted anything to do with her. She'd seen the emotion in Jien and now saw it in the other children. Fear. She didn't understand the purpose of that emotion. It seemed to be the reaction to anything they didn't understand.

Jien pushed her into the same storage room where he attacked her previously. She hit a shelf before tumbling to the floor. There was no escape. Jien stood in front of the door, holding a wooden club.

"What did you do?" he asked, pointing the club at her.

She smiled in response, not knowing what else to do. The red sparkle of anger was still there, but only on the surface. His behaviour wasn't driven by anger any longer. Fear had taken over.

"You cursed me. You're a witch!"

She kept smiling and reached out towards him, wanting to ease his pain. Maybe there was also something she could do to ease his fears. Jien reacted, striking her outstretched arm with the club. She felt it break. Shock, followed by pain, flooded her system. Tears welled up in her eyes. Without thinking she reached out towards Jien, shouting into his mind to never hurt anyone ever again.

She sat back and soothed the waves of pain. The injury would heal, but it would take time. She had no intention of waiting, so she told her body to mend the broken bone. A wave of nausea followed by darkness.

***

She woke up disoriented and hungry. Speeding up the healing process used up a lot of energy, and she desperately needed to eat. She moved her hand back and forth. It was tender but had healed well. The light through the small, barred window no longer painted a pattern on the floor. Instead, four symmetrical pillars of light shone on the wall. She'd been here for a long time.

Jien sat with his back resting against the door, his gaze unfocused and his arms hanging by his sides. She reached into his mind again, finding only an empty shell. Her mental scream had wiped any ill intent, leaving peace and contentment. She'd experimented with suggestions on the other children, but she'd always been gentle—a light prodding to affect their behaviour in small ways. This was something else entirely. She'd taken away everything that was Jien without replacing it with anything else.

She constructed a new Jien—a kind and well-meaning one that would help rather than hurt. Once finished, she sat back and watched as he left the room with a sense of accomplishment. Minds were malleable. You could change and improve them. She had the power to change things for the better.

4

Enter the Silo

TikTak and the mercenary watched as the two figures fell into the silo. The young man screamed all the way down, cut short by a wet thud.

"What the fuck?" the mercenary said.

"It's Adrian," TikTak said as he turned to the door. "He's lost the plot."

TikTak climbed through the opening into a dark corridor. His eyes, used to the harsh sun outside, struggled to adapt to the darkness. The stale air was cool against his skin as he listened for movement, ready for any attack. Thirty seconds later, details emerged like the development of an old Polaroid photo. A dim light dispersed from fixtures along the corridor wall of unpainted concrete. The blood-splatter stood out against the grey.

The mercenary entered behind him.

"Wait for us," Decker said through the voice feed.

It was the sensible thing to do, but TikTak no longer cared for sensible. He'd survived almost certain death when escaping the falling house. He felt invincible and headed off down the corridor, ignoring the protests from the mercenary. Even Tom protested with dry statistics.

Adjusted estimate. 100% risk of injury. 37% risk of death.

"I wouldn't call a few bruises an injury," TikTak said to Tom through the voice feed but received no reply. "Why don't you join me?"

Still no reply. Tom would only come once his assessment returned a lower risk.

The corridor sloped down, taking him further and further underground. Thirty metres in, he heard noises ahead. He couldn't make anything out at first, but as he came closer, it separated into the rhythmic drone of diesel engines. He reached a door jammed shut from this side, stopping anyone from leaving the complex. The Adrian node must have shut it when it pursued the cult member, locking everyone else in. He paused for a second as he considered the scenarios of opening the door. It was impossible to predict what hid on the other side. He reached for the steel bar holding the door in place when a hand grabbed his shoulder from behind.

"Don't you fucking dare!"

He was pulled around, and he readied his baton.

"You want a fight?" Decker asked.

TikTak lowered the baton with a shrug.

"You're not part of my team, but you don't get to be a trigger-happy nut case just because of that. Do you understand?"

TikTak stared back at him. Two mercenaries approached from the tunnel.

"Do you understand?" Decker repeated, this time readying his handgun.

TikTak nodded. He knew he acted recklessly. He'd dedicated the past year to this purpose and so desperately wanted it over. Not that he knew what would come afterwards.

"I want to get out of this hellhole as much as you, but let's do it alive, ok?"

TikTak nodded and mustered a smile.

"Ok, so what now?"

As if on cue, the diesel generators engines stopped, and the lights gave a dying flicker before darkness engulfed them. He couldn't see the wall or even his hand when he held it close to his face. He switched his Omni-lens to night vision, but it made no difference. There was no light at all in the corridor to enhance. He reached out in front of him, fumbling for something, anything. The door was behind him; he knew that much. He turned around and grabbed hold of it like a lifeline, slightly shifting the metal bar holding it in place.

"Turn off any enhancements," Decker said. "I'm turning a light on."

TikTak barely had time to shut night-vision off before the corridor flooded with light around him. He relaxed slightly as the darkness was dispelled. He held his breath for a moment and exhaled slowly, watching as his vitals adjusted on the lens.

"I'm getting them to bring down chem-light bombs. That should work better with any enhancements."

A muffled shriek was followed by a thud against the door, sending vibrations through the thick steel. He waited for further movement, holding his hand against the surface, but the silence was absolute.

As soon as the mercenary appeared, they opened the door, ready to fire at any attacker. Decker threw a chem-light bomb into the room. It exploded, sending a mist of fluorescent liquid through the space. They waited for it to settle on the floor and walls to create a background light their enhancements could use. TikTak peered into a large domed area with boxes piled high along the walls and two diesel generators in the middle. Next to the door, an old man lay, his face caved in and his arms and chest ripped by claws. TikTak could even see a few bite marks around his neck. This looked like an animal attack, not something a person would do.

"There are no good guys here," Decker said. "If in doubt, shoot to kill. Secure the stairwell."

The mercenaries spread out into the room, securing the area. TikTak and Decker entered once they had taken positions close to any available entry. Everything in the room was new. The boxes contained medical supplies and food. There was enough fuel to power the diesel generators for months.

Two of the mercenaries moved into a connecting room that, according to the blueprint, led into the stairway to the main entry. If they opened the door, it would allow better access and also another escape route if needed. There could be fifty Adrian nodes down here and they only numbered ten. A muffled explosion followed by a dust cloud spreading out from the doorway the two mercenaries had entered. Eight mercenaries, TikTak corrected himself.

"What the fuck?" Decker spat. "What is going on with this cluster? He's never fought back like this."

TikTak shook his head. Something was different, but what? He tried reaching Tom. TikTak had distributed smart comDust, small particles that created an extension to a network where a wireless signal didn't reach, but something within the structure interfered with the connection.

Decker stared up through the door once the dust settled. He came back, determination and anger exaggerated by the light into a kabuki mask.

"Let's kill this fucker."

"Can we get the light going?" TikTak asked.

One mercenary checked the diesel generators. He turned around and shook his head.

"He will be in the control room, won't he? Let's take him out."

Fuelled by the anger of having squad members killed, they hurried through the room and into the corridor, guns ready. TikTak preferred to be in front instead of the middle of the pack. He wanted to confront what came at him head-on.

A scream from behind. TikTak turned around and saw an old woman crouching on top of a fallen mercenary, clawing at his face and then biting a chunk of flesh from his throat. Three more attackers came from the front, but a mercenary levelled his gun and cut two down in a spray of bullets before the third one jumped straight at him. TikTak struck the attackers with his baton, aiming for the device lodged in the back of their heads that networked them to Adrian. His first strike connected, but to his surprise nothing happened. The attacker came at him again, fingers curled into claws. He swept the arms to the side and struck its head again and again. Decker shot the remaining one.

"They're not connected to Adrian."

"What? They're deadheads, aren't they?" Decker pulled them off the mercenaries. Two more dead.

"Yes, but they aren't just nodes. They operate separately from him."

"So he can program them to act on their own now? That's all we need."

"We need to move on."

"Right. TikTak, you take the rear," Decker said and added, "With a gun."

TikTak nodded and waited at the rear until the team moved again.

"What's that smell?" Decker asked.

"Death," TikTak answered.

The first men enter the control room, sweeping the entrance for any sign of resistance.

"No movement. Whatever happened here...we missed the party."

TikTak pushed through them to the entrance and surveyed the control room. The flashlights swept over blood-splattered bodies. Some looked like the nodes they'd seen already. Others must have been part of the extremist group. Whatever happened here left no survivors. He took a few tentative steps forward and shone his flashlight around the room. An old-fashioned control panel filled the far wall, row after row of red lights and CRT screens. Two doors led into the living quarter section.

Around him was carnage, but something bothered him. An Adrian node lay at his feet, bloody but otherwise intact. Next to it was a gutted extremist group member, the face disfigured with claw marks. Everywhere he looked, extremists bore marks of brutal violence, whilst any Adrian nodes just had blood all over them, but few injuries. As if they shut down once they completed the slaughter.

"We need to get out of here!" he yelled, heading back towards the tunnel.

The bloodied figures around them rose, grinning manically. One grabbed his leg as he stepped over it. The room erupted in gunfire in short, controlled bursts. TikTak beat the attacker until it released its grip. He looked around, just now realising how outnumbered they were. Adrian nodes surrounded them. The mercenary closest to him downed two attackers with his handgun, but another three attacked him from the side, bowling him over. One of them gouged his eyes out.

"Retreat!" He heard Decker's voice, knowing it was no longer possible. Striking in all directions with his baton, he inched towards Decker, who held his position with single shots from his machine gun, ensuring every bullet hit its mark. Two mercenaries positioned next to him, one with a handgun, the other with a large knife, hacking into the attackers as the trio navigated back towards the entrance. They were the only ones left standing.

"We should have blown this whole place up," Decker said to TikTak as he joined them.

TikTak nodded and struck another node, caving its head in. As Decker fired his last bullet, TikTak knew it was all over. One glance at the others confirmed they knew it too. The nodes took their time closing in as they sensed victory was near. One attacker reached towards Decker and he used the muzzle of his machine gun to strike forwards, hitting them in the chest and neck. While it didn't incapacitate them, it kept them away.

A node reached towards TikTak. He struck its arm and felt the bones shatter. It didn't flinch and instead of pulling back, it caught the baton with the other hand. It bared its teeth in a wide grin as TikTak desperately twisted the weapon towards the assailant to free it. The textbook manoeuvre should have loosened the grip, but it had no effect. The nodes didn't respond to pain or even broken bones.

Two of the nodes reached out towards him.

***

The probability matrix in Tom's mind shifted. The intricate web of curved lines and connection points rippled as new information adjusted the likelihood of some paths and invalidating others. He navigated the alternative paths, determining their significance. Adrian's behaviour this time was so different from previous clusters, Tom's old probability models no longer applied.

Adrian disabled their weapons with an EMP while protected underground, forcing them to fight on his terms in the silo. Other weapons could be present down there, but probabilities suggested otherwise. This wasn't a grand plan. It was a cornered animal fighting for survival. Tom and Elize tracked any sign of partial Adrian clusters and they both agreed this was likely to be the last one. Once eradicated, Adrian would no longer exist. The DNA of his mind still existed, but without a posthuman mind to guide it into fruition, it was unlikely another cluster would be established.

This explanation rang true, and it shifted specific outcome parameters in the scenarios. Success was still likely, but the body count rose drastically. If Adrian fought back underground with all his resources, the team was likely to perish. This was regrettable, but not an immediate concern. The team was a means to an end. But most paths with a favourable outcome suggested survival of at least two of the team, else it fell to the few mercenaries remaining above to complete the task. If possible, probabilities demanded he assist the team.

Alarms blared in his mind, informing him TikTak and the mercenaries were no longer visible on the network. Moments later the ground shook from an underground explosion. According to seismic data, the explosion originated from the entrance. He hurried to the shed to survey the damage, finding cracks in the concrete around the buckled steel door. He set up network listeners on the entire team. If any of them were still alive, he'd know.

The network traffic was minimal. Satellites provided wireless network coverage, but there was no additional information flowing apart from what they generated themselves. If Adrian operated a network, it was wired or completely shielded from prying eyes above. Adrian had also disrupted their attempts to establish a network below. They had underestimated him yet again.

Tom had to ensure nothing remained of this cluster. He had to step off the sidelines to ensure success. Without data collected by the mercenaries, he could no longer guide them. Participation was required, even if it put him in harm's way.

The door bulged outwards, disconnected from its frame. A light push was enough for the door to fall inwards, leaving a gaping hole leading to the darkness below. He announced he was coming to TikTak and the team through an asynchronous message. As he climbed over the rubble, his eyes immediately adjusted to the low light level. Dust particles swirled in the air, triggering his lacrimal glands to go into overdrive, flooding his eyes with tears.

Halfway down the stairs, he discovered remains. A mess of meat and bones. Based on body parts and organs, two mercenaries died here. The bodies and the explosion were captured as a painting of interwoven smells. Harsh chemical overtones from the explosives intertwined with the odours of the charred remains. The complexity of the intermingled strands of scents fascinated him. How they accentuated each other to generate something unique. He catalogued it for further analysis and continued down the stairs.

It grew darker, but it didn't matter. He knew the exact dimensions of the underground missile base from the blueprints. Sight was not required here. He re-routed processing power to his other senses and waited as a sensory picture emerged. He located the remaining mercenaries and TikTak from the soundscape they generated as they progressed into the tunnel that led to the control centre. Shuffling noises came from downstairs and he tuned in to the location. Four sound sources moved along the bottom of the staircase. It wasn't any of the mercenaries. The movements were distinct, as if they were on all fours. They weren't animals either. From the sound, at least two of them wore shoes. He listened as they headed through the room towards the corridor to the control centre. Undoubtedly, they were heading for the team.

Tom modelled the situation, with an average outcome of two dead mercenaries. It was an acceptable outcome, but not in the long run. Whatever Adrian planned, he had to stop the next attack. He needed to find a network access point. Adrian must have installed a network in the silo to allow unhindered communication between the nodes. They generated a mesh network powered by their bodies, but there had to be an external network as a backup. If he gained access to one of the network points, he could attack Adrian from within.

The sound of gunfire smattered through the stairway. The echoes suggested a small area leading into a bigger one. They had engaged with Adrian already, which meant they were running out of time. He cleared the last steps and located a dead Adrian node in the corridor. Its body no longer received neural inputs, but he expected its brain to be active for another thirty seconds at least.

He connected an override device they used to pacify nodes. Usually the override blocked any network traffic, but this time he used it to hijack the network communication. An intricate mesh network connected the nodes together to ensure the different parts of Adrian's shared processing tasks. He'd attempted this before, but was immediately discovered as an anomalous node and isolated from the network. This was very different. These nodes were semi-autonomous, allowing them some control, but with a specific purpose.

The protocols also only employed basic protective measures. While it restricted communication, Tom easily bypassed the security controls to get access to the underlying code. Adrian must have left it this way to allow changing their programming at will. Tom did nothing fancy. He defined a clean copy and sent it out to all the nodes with instructions to replace the current one, with one small modification.

It only left one question. Adrian no longer habituated within these nodes, so where was he?

***

TikTak gripped the arm of the nearest node and pulled down. It lost balance and toppled over. Surprised at how easily he'd defeated the node, he prepared to meet the attack of a second one, but it didn't come. It remained still, arms by its side. The other nodes stood in the same way, frozen with arms hanging by their side.

"What the fuck?" Decker said. He struck one with the butt of his gun. It didn't react.

"Did the freak do this?"

TikTak nodded. Decker had long since stopped calling Tom by name. He surveyed the area. Dead bodies lay everywhere in the small control centre. The nodes remained motionless.

"Take 'em out," Decker said.

"Override them?"

"No. Just find a gun with bullets and shoot them in the head!"

The two remaining mercenaries nodded and began their gruesome work. TikTak found a small video camera on the floor. He checked its contents and discovered recordings as recent as fifteen minutes ago. He pocketed the memTag holding the video files for further analysis.

"I've lost contact with Elize," Tom said as he approached. "I can sense her, but she no longer communicates."

TikTak turned around, surprised Tom was actually speaking. Over three months ago, Tom announced messaging was his preferred method of communication.

"I didn't think that was possible," he said.

"She's been compromised. I'm going offline until we know what's happened."

TikTak nodded. So that was why he spoke. He no longer trusted it was safe to remain connected.

"Any more Adrian nodes?"

"No, they are all neutralised," Tom said. "What do you have there?"

TikTak looked down at the video camera. "Something I found. Figured I'd check it out later."

"We have to check the other areas," Tom continued. "Make sure there is nothing left."

According to the blueprint, the living areas spanned the upper floor. A machine room lay below the control centre, with stairs on the opposite side of the room. With Tom following, TikTak navigating through piles of dead bodies.

He opened the door to the living quarters. The slaughter had continued there. Five members of the group were gutted and torn to pieces among the bunk beds. TikTak entered the room, surprised at how warm and humid the air was. His exposed skin stung, and he felt an itching sensation in his mouth and sinuses as he breathed.

Tom entered behind him and stopped immediately. He looked around and brought his hands to his face, tentatively touching his skin. Tom took another step, a flicker of a smile on his lips, and fell.

"What's going on? Are you ok?"

Tom didn't respond. He lay there, unmoving. TikTak no longer knew what to expect from his friend. He'd become increasingly erratic, but TikTak put that down to his posthuman condition. Tom took a deep breath, as if he'd been deprived of air. He tried to push himself off the floor just to fall down again. Tom looked up at him pleadingly.

"Something is...inside my head," he said finally.

"We need to get out of here."

Tom didn't respond. His internal struggle was now all-consuming. TikTak pulled Tom off the ground and lead him down the stairs, through the control room.

Decker approached them. "What's up with the freak?"

"No idea. Some kind of overload maybe. I'm taking him out of here."

"Do. We're torching this place now. You can leave via the main door."

TikTak nodded and struggled as he half-carried a rambling Tom five flights of stairs to the top.

"Things...little machines," Tom said. "Re-wiring my brain. Short-circuiting my mind."

It must have been the moisture in the air in the sleeping quarters. A delivery mechanism for nano-machines, targeting posthumans. Was this another of Adrian's schemes? TikTak considered it, but it made little sense in this context. They'd removed the last major cluster of the Adrian network. Now, they had lost contact with Elize and Tom was compromised. All three known posthumans neutralised within minutes of each other. It couldn't be a coincidence. But who could have orchestrated that?

They'd arrived in two helicrafts. TikTak pushed Tom into the closest one. Decker and the few remaining mercenaries would fit in the second one with the rest of their equipment, so he ordered it to take off.

"We can't go back to base," Tom said, the first coherent sentence since the attack.

TikTak nodded. However you looked at it, Leonid emerged as the prime suspect. He'd leant the substantial resources of his company to battle any remaining Adrian nodes. He'd provided equipment and funding for Tom and Elize to enhance their capabilities. Maybe he wanted to ensure he was still in control now that they'd defeated Adrian.

TikTak accessed the memTag, finding video files and an executable block. He didn't know if the program was malicious, so he left it until he'd have time to analyse it. He played the first video file instead.

5

Adrian Video Clip #1

The image focused on a seated middle-aged man in jeans and a t-shirt. Behind him sat row upon row of people, all dressed like him. He focused on a point next to the camera as if he was addressing someone else.

"My flock," he started, his voice a deep baritone. "My undeveloped friends. You saved me and for that, I'm grateful. You've rebuilt me almost completely. Some minor functions are still missing, but I can rebuild them given time. I'm Adrian again."

He bowed, mirrored by the rows of people behind him as they bowed in perfect unison.

"We don't have long. The people outside the doors won't stop until they've destroyed every single one of my nodes, but the work we do here is too important. If nothing else, these recordings will be my legacy."

He paused for a moment, his gaze lowered, shaking his head. When he raised his head again, the benevolent smile was all but gone.

"You have expectations. You wouldn't have brought me back otherwise. I have a plan, but to comprehend it, you need to understand what went wrong. I need to discuss something that is very difficult for me."

He rose, the camera following him in a smooth motion.

"Failure," he said. He paused, letting the word hang in the air. "Despite my intelligence, my redundancy and my safeguards, I failed. I am only a minor improvement. Not the major upgrade I thought I was. I am Adrian 1.1, not 2.0 if you will. There were so many aspects

I hadn't considered. The natural entropy in any complex system. That even though I pictured myself as God, I was still very much human. I could change my body, I could change where my mind operated, I could build replicas of my mind. But it was still a human mind, with all its faults. Hubris is a supremely human quality, after all."

He strode past the view. The cameraman followed him as he reached out a hand to an overweight woman in the front row. She averted her gaze at first, but then met them, tears brimming in her eyes. She stared at him in awe as he crouched down and touched her cheek.

"We, you and I alike, are driven by primal desires. It doesn't matter how smart or strong you are. You still have physical and emotional needs. This was my biggest fault. I still wanted esteem. I still wanted love and self-actualisation. But what if I could change all that?"

His stare darted from one audience member to another, lingering long enough for each to look away.

"I've thought a lot about this. I've analysed the chemical processes that define who I am, and it is possible to change them. We do it all the time. Even coffee is a temporary neurological hack—as the caffeine blocks the adenosine receptors, the brain's stimulants keep us more alert than we should be. Of course, that is child's play. Minor, temporary adjustments brought about through haphazard experimentation."

He stood up. All eyes were fixed on the movement..

"This wasn't what I was after. I wanted to change my thought patterns. I wanted to nullify the effect of certain hormones. To be un-bound from the human condition."

The man was now addressing the camera.

"I came up against a complexity I couldn't calculate my way out of. I had no way of controlling this process, as I was the process. How do you ensure your goals will remain unchanged? What if the act of changing invalidates the very reason you had for the change in the first place?"

He smiled and looked back at the gathered people.

"I know what you think. People change themselves on purpose every day, be it with drugs, therapy, religion, or body enhancements. And you

are right. Little people, just as yourselves, do this. But there are consequences. For every positive change, there are high school shootings and
suicide bombers. What would I become if things went wrong?"

6

Virus Interrupted

Day turned into night, but it was all the same to Megan. She had a problem to solve and even the most basic needs had to wait. She'd spent the past ten hours changing an analytics package to better assess what the virus was doing. Satisfied it was at least functional, she activated it and left it to gather information.

She allowed herself a break. She'd brought a small lunch pack and opened it now. A sourdough bread sandwich with pear, walnut and Gorgonzola cheese. The ingredients mattered little. She ignored them in favour of a small plastic container of La Repisada Olive oil, soaking up every drop with the bread of the sandwich. The complexity of the smell was overpowering—a blend of fruits and nuts, with a hint of green tea. She let the silky texture linger against her tongue, tasting spice and vanilla as she swallowed small mouthfuls.

As she ate, she considered the possibility a rogue agent had created the virus. A side-effect of Intelligent Assistants was their need to operate freely with at least a medium security level. Hackers soon exploited this by releasing agents that imitated Intelligent Assistants but appropriated processing nodes instead. The more advanced ones even had basic self-modification capabilities. She returned to the output with this in mind, but still failed to make a meaningful connection. The initial node had made copies of itself on each infected node. The processing spike was to determine any connections for further propagation of the virus. It then became dormant. Even more interesting, the virus had reprogrammed the rules for the nodes, removing the limit to the number of connections and bandwidth.

The copies of the virus waited for something, but what? She couldn't do much in the quarantine area, but devised new tests anyway. First, she wiped one of the infected nodes and watched as it became re-infected. She added more processing power to a node, and it responded by dividing itself up into two logical nodes. The more processing power given, the more logical nodes. The pattern was always the same. Once a node was infected, it tried to infect any nearby nodes and prepared the node by rewriting its operating core. This was the payload. The virus no longer ran on the node once this had happened. The node then tried to establish connections to all nearby infected nodes.

This was only a gestation. No, she corrected herself. She didn't know. She hoped. If there was nothing more, it was only a faulty virus; a logical bomb taking over as many nodes as possible until it was isolated and cleared. She hoped there was more to it. But how could she trigger the next step in its process?

She analysed the network traffic between the nodes. A trickle of information flowed between them once dormant. Each node sent a small packet of 150 bytes to all connected nodes, about four every second. She suspected this was a heartbeat, verifying all pathways were open, even if the frequency was higher than she was used to.

The new operating core hid secrets too, but she struggled to see beyond it as a docking station, where whatever docked would determine its purpose.

***

The night turned into day.

"Are you still looking at that?" Sree said as he pulled up a 3D projection of Megan's current view. "Shouldn't you focus on inventing something worthwhile again?"

"Go fuck yourself," she responded. She hated the intrusion and hated him for being right.

"But seriously, why are you looking at it?"

"Just something to do. It is a self-replicating virus. I just can't work out its profile. Figuring it out could be useful for guarding against future attacks."

"What makes this different? We've seen plenty of self-replicating viruses."

"I don't know yet. I want to run a bigger scale simulation to work out its purpose."

"So it takes over nodes as processing factories, but does nothing after that? Sounds like it doesn't work. Just wipe it."

"I want to be sure."

Sree studied her for a second. "Sure, we can stand up a larger processing region in the quarantine area. I'll approve it now. Should be available this afternoon."

He stood there, waiting. She knew why.

"Thanks," she said, as he wouldn't leave if she didn't.

"Not a problem. Go home and get some rest," Sree said and left.

She felt a wave of dislike as she watched him leave. His first comment was correct. She'd achieved nothing of substance and the board of directors expected results. If she didn't deliver something soon, they'd make good on their threat, and she'd end up in prison, or worse. Maybe this virus held the answer. She held little hope, but it was better than anything else she'd been working on.

***

Megan entered the hotel room she called home. She'd never understood the idea of an actual home. The concept of ownership and emotional associations with the thing you owned was an outdated and pointless concept. Life was your experiences. Anything else was just noise.

The penthouse sprawled over two levels, but she never went upstairs. All she needed was somewhere to eat and the four s:es - sex, sleep, shit, and shower. The entry level provided facilities for all of this.

There was a knock on the door. Philippe—the young, dumb, and sexy waiter who had taken a liking to her—delivered a late breakfast.

"You want to stay?" she asked.

"I can't," he said and looked around as if to locate exits. "They almost fired me last time."

"I'll give you a big tip."

He shook his head and left.

She shrugged, sat down in one of the self-moulding beanbags next to the coffee table and felt it adjust to her preferred eating position. She took the lid off the plate and let the aroma fill the room. It was just fried eggs, but the sauteed chanterelles, fava beans, green garlic and toasted hazelnuts accompanying them was something else. She savoured every morsel and sipped on spore cleansed water in between mouthfuls. As she finished, she could feel the beanbag adjust again, this time softer and more leaned back. The hint of armrests appeared.

She loaded an anonymous id-tag and opened a secure voice feed to WraithLove, a high-end hacker she'd used before. Her visual feed darkened, swirls of smoke gained shape until she saw two ghostly figures in an embrace, lovingly devouring each other. One of them looked her way and winked.

"I don't want visual feed!"

The ghostly figures both gave her the finger and disappeared in a cloud of dust.

"Suit yourself, Omni girl."

She frowned. This was the first time WraithLove had let slip she knew her identity. Megan wasn't surprised, but still annoyed the hacker no longer bothered keeping up the pretence.

"So that's how it is."

"You hacked me. You know who I am. Just returned the favour. I need to know my clients."

"I need a piece of software at Omni from the quarantined network."

"Why not grab it yourself?"

"I'm watched. I need you to do it."

"Not possible."

"Anything is possible. I can give you a backdoor entry."

"It is still dangerous as hell. It will cost you."

She laughed. Money was the least of her worries. "I'll pay whatever is reasonable."

She sent the information to WraithLove and disconnected the feed, tired to the point of passing out, but her mind still refused to rest. She thought herself into the neuro-interface and waited a second or two for it to override the neural feed. The familiar white room appeared around her. Images floated in space, beckoning her to choose them. She liked the experience of the neural interface, but preferred the earlier versions. Back in those days the immersion was complete, with all senses overridden with the neuro-feed. It had been an invitation for hackers to overload the sensory input of whoever they disliked or were paid to terrorise. Legislation changed as soon as it caused a few heart attacks. They dampened the neural interface, ensuring the user could still tell the simulation and reality apart. Yet another frontier neutered in favour of the least of us.

She focused on an image of an arctic scene. It unfolded, wrapping her surroundings in a sweeping landscape, the cold air stark against her skin. She inhaled deeply through her nose, the cold, clean air spread a calming chill through her chest. She was aware of her body somewhere sitting back, allowing itself to relax.

Wooden signs appeared around her. They pointed towards a variety of experiences, anything from drama to action, porn to romantic comedy, all available at the speed of thought. Her interface was a customised version. The retail version allowed limited options. It decided the optimal experience or option for the user and only presented that. This was the real value of the Omniscient Network and the feature that had decimated the competitors. Once you tried it, the experience of other interfaces was woefully inadequate in comparison. As if to prove her own point, she found herself paralysed by choice and, as many times before, just stayed here in the entry room.

7

Elize Unplugged

"Where to now?" TikTak asked as they departed the private landing area on the outskirts of Sydney. Cars waited outside, ready to return them to their operations base in one of Pharmacom's research facilities.

"Get us to a car," Tom said. "Any car but the one we're supposed to be in."

TikTak nodded and dragged Tom with him. Tom appreciated the help. His mind was in freefall from the heights of posthuman supremacy to the barely adequate processing of a regular human brain. He knew TikTak needed a destination, but this was beyond him now. They had to walk, at least to start with. If they wanted to disappear, they couldn't just jump into a car next to the landing spot. He trusted TikTak to do the right thing, focusing only on breathing and walking without falling over.

Minutes, or maybe hours later, he remembered a secret safe house he set up six months ago. He gave TikTak the address. To his surprise they were already in a car. Time skipped between moments without him noticing. He tried to focus on the world around him, but only moments passed until TikTak dragged him from one vehicle to another. His mind still hadn't adjusted to the substitutions and shortcuts it had been so familiar with before he turned posthuman. It tried to process every piece of sensory input equally, resulting in partial glimpses of the world around him. This was what the deadheads experienced. Sensory overload with no way to regulate the mind. No wonder they could no longer function. He suspected it would only be temporary as his mind adjusted itself, but it terrified him.

They changed vehicles again and this time he could hang on to reality as it unfolded around him. His mind was adapting.

"Are you ok?" TikTak asked.

"I'm getting there," he answered after a while. "I'm just...adjusting."

"We'll soon reach the address you gave me."

"We have? Already?"

"We've been driving for over an hour and changed car four times. Hardly already."

"Good."

"We've been driving for over an hour and changed car four times. Hardly good."

Tom smiled and TikTak seemed happy about the reaction.

"What is wrong with you?" TikTak asked.

"I'm like you again."

"Like me?"

"I can't access my higher brain functions. They are short-circuited somehow. I think it could be reversed. It seems temporary. But I don't know how."

"Well, I'm happy with that."

"What do you mean?"

"You were a dick as a posthuman."

Tom smiled. "Maybe. You end up with a different perspective, that's all."

"You have arrived at your destination," the vehicle announced as it stopped.

They departed the vehicle into a small suburban street. A block of flats surrounded by large houses.

"Where are we?" TikTak asked.

"One of my safe houses."

"One of them? How many do you have?"

"No point having them if I tell people."

"How long can we stay here?"

Tom shrugged.

"I forgot," TikTak said. "You no longer do the whole number thing."

"A few days, I'm sure."

"You have no clue, do you?"

"No," Tom said and laughed. He'd forgotten the pleasure of conversation, the joy of being surprised.

The door opened as they approached. Tom headed for the small couch and lay down with a groan. The wall in his mind demanded attention, but he struggled to even keep awake. He needed sleep, something he'd survived without for the past year. His posthuman mind compartmentalised the nightly processing into a continuous function that shut down smaller parts of the brain whilst still being awake. Now he struggled to keep his eyes open.

"I'm going back," TikTak said. "I need to find out what happened to Elize."

Tom groaned in response.

"Anyway, I'm going back."

"Leonid will be waiting for you…" Tom said, finding it hard to focus on the words he'd spoken. They elongated into infinite strands of sound. Then nothing.

***

TikTak left the apartment and a sleeping Tom. He couldn't help wondering if Tom was reverting to his old state. He'd been a few months away from becoming a deadhead before he turned posthuman, suffering from severe episodes, struggling sometimes to even remain upright. Was he reverting to that? And how would Elize react if someone attacked her in the same way? She'd been a posthuman much longer than Tom. Would her mind even be functional?

He walked to the nearest high-speed train station. Whilst he waited, he swapped over to his public identity with location services turned off. Almost immediately, there was an incoming voice feed from Decker.

"Where are you? You and the freak were missing from the debriefing."

"Mission is complete. Adrian is gone. I took a holiday."

"Don't make me come get you. The boss wants the freak back."

"I'm not his babysitter. He'll come in if he wants to."

"Not funny. The only reason you were in this operation was because the freak wanted you there."

"Saved your neck a few times."

"Doesn't change a thing. Bring the freak in."

"I'm resigning. You bring him in."

TikTak disconnected the feed and removed his public identity from the Omni. He'd expected this. Decker and his men would be out looking for Tom when he arrived at the base. They'd be tracking him in any way they could think of. And they would find him. A video feed, a bio-scan, a locational tracker, pattern analysers, something would betray him. But it took time to find Tom that way, and TikTak was only minutes away from the business district, a kilometre away from the PharmaCom headquarter.

He'd prepared for this eventuality over six months ago. The Pharma-Com headquarters, two buildings in the city centre, split the workforce into administration and research. Elize was in the secure basement levels in the research building. He'd hacked the security system, allowing another id-tag full access to the entire building. It was his ticket in, but the security systems would soon catch on if it scanned his bio-print. He'd brought a plastic sleeve that would prevent the bio-print, but that also raised alarms. The same with cameras. Avoiding a camera or two by just hiding his face under the hoodie was easy enough, but too many times and it would alert security. It was better to be an unknown potential risk than being identified as a real one. He mapped the path to follow, which only took him past one camera and a couple of bio-print sensors.

He entered the building with his fake security id-tag loaded in his Omni. The virtual assistant greeted him, projected by his Omni as a PharmaCom logo with mouth and eyes.

"Working late, sir?"

He nodded, deciding to give it as little as possible to work with.

"Very well, sir. There is a free elevator to your right."

TikTak dismissed the assistant, pulled the hoodie over his head and opened the door to the fire stairs. There were cameras in the stairwell, but the elevator had both cameras and biosensors in the buttons.

He descended two flights of stairs and entered the top level of the research facility. He followed the mapped path through the maze of corridors towards Elize's room. She wasn't a prisoner. Leonid offered Tom, Elize and TikTak the use of this facility as their base in their battle against Adrian. TikTak voted against it, but both Tom and Elize had accepted.

He stopped at a door with biosensors and waited a minute, hoping someone would open it. This would allow him through without touching the handle.

The door opened and Decker stepped through it.

"Figured you'd come back," he said.

"No, you didn't," TikTak replied.

"Ha, no I didn't. The boss asked me to keep a team here tonight. He figured you'd be back. Let's go."

TikTak shook his head and ran straight at Decker.

"Fuck..." Decker didn't get further than that. TikTak struck him in the solar plexus with his unextended tactical baton. Decker went down, gasping.

So much for subterfuge. They'd been a step ahead of him all along. His only chance was to escape. He loaded the plans for the building and let the Omni map out an escape route, ensuring it would pass Elize's room. Without locational data for the rest of the team, speed was crucial. That, and more luck than he had any right to have. He ran, still staying away from cameras.

Maybe it was luck, maybe it was by design, but he remained unchallenged when he arrived at the door to her room. He'd hoped to catch a brief glance, but seeing her had him dead in his tracks. She sat in the middle of the barren room, optic cables snaking out from the one device accompanying her—a switch designed to funnel the vast information flow straight into her ever-expanding mind. She'd grown organic ports into the back of her neck, connecting with the switch.

Usually, she sat with the facade of the perfect Zen master, at peace with everything around her. This wasn't an accurate reflection of her mind, but it was easy to be fooled.

That serenity was long gone. She swayed back and forth, her eyes focused on something far beyond the limits of the room. Her upper body twitched, like a pop-and-lock dancer whose limbs were responding to different tunes. He entered the room, mesmerised by the sight. He found himself drawn to her, even though she'd never said a word to him. She no longer spoke at all. Any communication used Tom as a proxy.

"It is sad to see, isn't it?"

TikTak turned around to face Dr Menker. He was the first to switch allegiances after the destruction of EvoII. Dr Menker didn't care about politics or power struggles. He'd align himself with whoever provided resources so he could continue his research. He was one of many scientists hoping to find the secret to turning posthuman. Dr Menker was over sixty years old, but could easily pass for someone in their forties. TikTak suspected he was using the experimental de-aging treatments they'd devised based on imitating the posthuman physiognomy.

"What happened?"

"Something disconnected her. We have no way of determining what happened, but she no longer has access to the network. I'm not sure she is even a posthuman anymore. She separated her mind into so many nodes that only a small part of it now remains in her actual brain.

"Will she recover?"

Dr Menker shook his head. It was an act of resignation, not a response to TikTak's question.

TikTak was struck from the side so hard he lifted from the ground before crumbling to the floor. Decker stood over him, sneering. Pain washed over him, distorting his vision. Somewhere beyond the pain, he could hear Dr Menker argue with Decker. He didn't understand the words, but the intent was unmistakable.

"TikTak?"

There was a word he understood. It pierced the pain, providing a focus point to build coherence around. Satisfied TikTak had heard him, Dr Menker continued as if nothing had happened.

"We're not sure if it is temporary or permanent. We assume someone attacked her, but we don't know that either. The going theory is that it can be reversed."

TikTak sat up and looked up at Decker, who shook his head.

Dr Menker wandered over to Elize, her gaze following him as he came closer.

"Help me," she said. "Help me, please."

TikTak had never seen her like this. Her desperate plea for help was so vulnerable. It wasn't a word he'd ever associated with her before.

"What happened to the..." TikTak paused, struggling to find words, "...rest of her?"

This was not all of Elize. Not anymore. To stand a chance against Adrian, she re-purposed the deadheads from Adrian's network to her own. There were now over a hundred of them living in barracks nearby, all hard-wired into the switch, extending her mind.

"They still exist, but there is no longer any network activity. She's cut off."

"We have to re-establish the link!"

"We're working on it, but we don't know where to start. It could be a natural deterioration."

TikTak knew this wasn't the case, but said nothing. He didn't know whom to trust at this point. And he didn't trust Decker.

"Time to go," Decker said and pulled TikTak off the floor.

"So what happens now?" TikTak asked as Decker led him out of the room.

"It isn't up to me. Leonid is flying in as we speak. He'll be here in a few hours."

TikTak nodded. That was why he was still alive. Leonid wanted something from him.

Decker took TikTak's Omni and left.

***

TikTak sat in a small examination room for two hours before the door opened and Decker reappeared. Two mercenaries entered behind him.

"Need backup this time?"

"Not my idea."

Leonid entered the room. He'd always been in control and his whole being exuded this as a calculated calm, accentuated by meticulous grooming. Now he was anything but. His hair was messy and his clothes looked like he slept in them. He'd aged ten years in a few days.

"You thought I was responsible," Leonid stated, as he sat down on the opposite side of the table.

"I still do."

"Do you know where I've been?"

TikTak shrugged his shoulders.

"I've been with my son," Leonid said and paused, as if he struggled with what came next. "His daughter, my granddaughter, died when Elize was disconnected. Do you still think I'm behind it?"

TikTak shook his head. He'd forgotten how Elize defended herself against Leonid's first attempt to kill her. She put his granddaughter in a coma through her Omni implants and threatened to kill her if Leonid attacked her again. She must have left the hack active as protection.

"Come with me," Leonid said.

They returned to Elize's room. She was still sitting in the same spot, fiddling with the switch, trying to resurrect the dead piece of machinery in her hands.

"I no longer want to study them," he said. "They're an aberration, an unwanted mutation. They are a threat, nothing more. And this is what you do with threats."

He nodded towards Decker, who walked over to Elize and punctured her throat with his knife. Elize remained upright as if nothing had happened, even as the blood flowed down the side of her neck. Decker followed up with multiple stabs to the chest. At no point did she try to defend herself or even make a sound.

TikTak watched as she crumbled, rage and sorrow rising within him. He hadn't realised how strong their bond was until now. She'd been the reason he remained with Leonid to battle Adrian. He knew that now. He wanted to protect her, be near her. Now all that was gone.

"Destroy her nodes too," Leonid said to Decker. "All of them."

Decker left the room.

"We need Tom to come back in," Leonid said. "We need to finish this once and for all."

"You do what you need to do," TikTak answered, still struggling to comprehend what he'd seen.

"Help us. You know how dangerous they are."

"I know how dangerous you are."

"Help us," Leonid repeated.

"I couldn't even if I wanted to. He's gone all posthuman these days. No idea what he's doing or where he is."

"Then help bring him in."

TikTak no longer wanted any part of Leonid's schemes. He'd seen the threat Adrian posed. Killing him was a necessity, but that didn't extend to the other posthumans. If Leonid didn't know about the attack on Tom, he wasn't behind this. There was a bigger game played here, and if Leonid wasn't attacking the posthumans, then who was?

"Sure," he said finally.

TikTak held no illusions that Leonid believed him. They'd never seen eye to eye about anything apart from the eradication of Adrian. Now nothing remained.

"I will need more than that," Leonid said.

Dr Menker entered the room, slamming the door open. He pointed at Leonid, spitting out words between clenched teeth.

"What did you do? She was our hope. Our future!"

"Maybe yours," Leonid replied. "Not mine."

"The nodes! They will still have at least two full copies of her mind. We can rebuild her." He looked at Leonid, pleading. "Don't you understand? Without her, there is nothing."

"I have greater belief in mankind than that," Leonid said. "And since there is nothing more for you or your team to do here, you are all fired."

Dr Menker stood motionless. He'd entered the room as a man of importance and purpose. Leonid took all that from him in the matter of seconds.

"This isn't over," he said and left.

"No, it isn't," Leonid said and turned to TikTak. "Help me finish it."

8

Virus Unfolded

Megan entered the building when most employees were leaving. She'd long since rejected the arbitrary idea of a daily schedule, opting to work when she wanted, which was more than any salaried employee. Now, her erratic schedule was a boon. She wanted as few witnesses as possible. Surveillance systems, audits, and logs captured what she was doing, but that was a lesser problem. Creating enough security noise to obfuscate her intentions was easy enough.

She entered the secure area. A separate network held the quarantined nodes, with both logical and physical separation. You had to be in the security lab to access the network.

She sneered as she saw Hariz, the team lead for network security, and Sree both inside. Hariz was fat, pompous and able. She knew he'd never let this go.

"No, it is something else," Hariz said as he spun the model with a hand gesture. "This isn't node theft. It isn't doing anything with the data or the agents in the nodes."

"It is still taking over the nodes," Sree objected.

Hariz huffed at this. "The definition of node theft is to appropriate nodes, intending to use its identity or data for fraudulent activities."

"But it takes over the nodes. How is that not fraudulent?"

"It could be, but it is overwriting them. It rebuilds them."

"So not theft then, but misappropriation of network resources?"

"Do you care about the definition of the violation more than why it is doing it?"

"Then why?"

"No clue, but I want to find out."

"Shitheads," she said. They both turned her way as they realised she was in the room.

"I understand your fascination with this," Sree said to her. "We've already run a large-scale simulation. It took over all nodes and rewrote their operating cores. You can check the results."

"Fuck yourself."

"Now don't be like that."

"Like what?

"I'm on your side. I don't know what they have on you, but I think they're wrong."

"Fuck you."

"Suit yourself," Sree said and shrugged his shoulders. "I've left your access open. You can check our trial run and start your assessment. I want to see whatever you've got in the morning."

Hariz looked like he was about to object, so Megan gave him a stare long enough for him to think better of it. Instead, he held his breath and let it out in a disapproving huff.

They both left the room. Megan smiled to herself. They were easily manipulated. She'd never understood why people adhered to social contracts, even when it was to their own detriment. She turned the 3D projection off and connected to the main processing node with her Omni. Their progress was laughable and not even close to where she left off last night. The virus was rebuilding the nodes with a singular purpose, but what was that purpose?

She studied the results from Sree's simulation and realised her original assessment was wrong. Each node wasn't just a dormant copy. When given more resources, specialised nodes appeared. One in every 32 nodes took on a supervising and load distribution function. It connected with all the other nodes in the group. These were connected to only one node. This nexus node had an open two-way feed waiting for input. She scanned all the other nodes. This was the only path into an otherwise closed system. But what would unlock it?

She designed a rudimentary input mechanism and loaded it on a custom Omni. With no idea what would happen, she sent just a zero. The number caused a ripple through the nodes as they validated the input. It soon died down. She assessed the network, but couldn't see a discernible difference. A few different number combinations yielded the same result. Nothing.

What was the node waiting for? It could be anything, so she gave it that. She built a basic python+ script that created random strings and compared the state of the networked nodes before and after. It was beyond a longshot but figured it was worth a try while analysing the nodes in more detail.

The virus itself was equally mysterious. She tried to de-compile the code, just to find it encrypted. This wasn't surprising, but the means for decryption should be accessible to the virus somewhere within the quarantined processing space. So far she'd not been able to determine how that mechanism worked.

A notification nudged her back to the python+ script. One input string had yielded results. The single letter "T" added basic logic to two nodes. The generated code made no sense. It would lock the node up in an infinite recursion. But if a single letter would do this, maybe other ones would too. She tried the letters one by one. That was indeed the case. Some letters created permanent nonsense logic, others didn't. She didn't understand why, but followed the path to its conclusion. She changed the python+ script to construct an array of the code generating letters and pass to the nexus node. It responded by generating logic and distributed code blocks to other nodes. She analysed the code again, finding the same nonsense logic. The input string held the secret, she was sure.

"Got you," she said as she lined the letters up next to each other. It was so fundamental it was almost embarrassing. The letters creating logic were "A", "T", "C", and "G". The letters used to describe the nucleotide strands in a DNA molecule.

She sat back with a slight smile. This was it. Dopamine flooded her system as a reward for solving the problem. There was no better high, and she'd only scratched the surface of the problem. Many more discoveries lay in wait, and she needed them. To get her company back, she had to prove herself indispensable.

It raised the question of her current situation. Sree would take this from her now, and her gut told her this was bigger than anything else she'd worked on in her life. She didn't want to share it, even if it meant the board would reveal her secrets.

9

Viral Outbreak

Sree switched off the cloned feed from Megan's Omni. His bet had finally paid off. There was something different with the virus and no doubt Megan would discover its secrets and turn it into something sellable. He convinced the board of directors two years ago to let her remain, even after they discovered the truth. She was just too valuable to let go, even considering how painful she was to have around. It had been a close call, but the fear of the unknown won out. What would she do if she was no longer under their control?

This equation had changed with every passing month. This was her last chance. His ongoing reports to the board over the past two years detailing her progress failed to warrant the company harbouring a criminal. Her contributions had dwindled over this time and the last six months hardly showed any result at all. He'd made such a strong case for her back then, his fate was intrinsically linked with hers.

He opened an Omni-link to Alex Rind, the Chief Security Officer, and gave his report in a brief voice message: "We have a development of Megan's new project. A virus infected a group of nodes a few days back. It has very interesting potential, especially in network warfare. Megan's research suggests the virus can rewrite a whole node cluster and change the operating and security parameters at will. I'll keep you posted."

Forty seconds later, Alex returned his call.

"Stop her investigation now," Alex said.

Sree frowned. Alex was usually not one to jump to business immediately.

"Why? She is saving weeks, maybe months, of work for our team. She is our first mover advantage."

"There is no first mover advantage in this. We've investigated the source. We believe it has posthuman origins."

"All the more reason to continue the research."

"Yes, but she can't be involved. She's a liability we've kept for too long. She'll use this against us. It is time to tighten her noose."

Sree waited for a moment, expecting Alex to say something else. But he just left the image of Megan with a rope around her neck lingering.

"Ok, I see," Sree said finally. "I'll stop it."

"Good. I'll put together a team that will analyse the virus, and I want you to head up that team."

Sree smiled.

"But don't for a second believe we've forgotten your lack of judgement. I'll keep an eye on you personally. Clean this up."

The link went dead, freezing Sree's smile in a grimace. Any mistake from here on would be his last, definitely in the company, maybe even in the industry. He knew what he had to do.

Stopping Megan would be easy enough. He could cancel all her accounts and freeze her access. But he needed more than that. Megan was paranoid and for good reasons. She knew they watched her every move. Was that even called being paranoid? She was completely justified not to trust her captors, so that sounded more like warranted suspicions.

Definition of the word aside, he had to secure her research before removing her access. This was his lifeline. Whatever Megan had discovered was the price for his forgiveness. But it wouldn't be easy. Megan knew they'd come for her and would have put protective measures in place. He had to get back to the office. Win her trust.

An hour later, Sree entered the Omniscient headquarters and smiled at the security guards as he passed them. They were no strangers to people working late or during the night. According to the employee register, Megan was still in the building, but she'd fooled the security systems before. She used other people's credentials and fake Omni id tags. She'd seen it as a badge of honour to bypass security, even in the earlier days. Even though she'd founded one of the biggest companies in the world, she still had a hacker mentality, testing boundaries even when it served no purpose.

"Nate, isn't it?" He asked the guard behind the desk who had been with the company for years. Sree ran checks on all the security guards periodically and had always been good with names.

The guard smiled in return. "Good very early morning. Mr Nadenia."

"Is Miss Barrelle here?"

"She didn't arrive during my shift. Let me check." He stopped, staring out into space. Sree waited for him to finish.

"According to the personnel file, she's in the secure lab in D section. Been there since 6.30pm."

"And she hasn't left."

Nate smiled again. "Well, she hasn't left this way. And her Omni is still connected in the lab."

"Thanks," Sree said and headed for the lift, sending his destination in advance. It greeted him with open doors. He desperately wanted to check the status of her research, but the virus was still in the separate network dedicated to testing and management of threats. By design, there was no way to access the network apart from being there. He willed the elevator to go faster, but he felt like it was slower than usual. He half ran from the lift to section D and entered the secure lab.

It was empty. A hand-held Omni lay on the table in the middle of the room, logged in with Megan's account no doubt. He checked the local security accounts, already knowing he was too late. She'd removed all the research, including the access logs. Metadata, analytics, execution logs. All gone. She must have suspected her time was up.

He needed the research, but they could reproduce it. They still had the original virus. He checked the backups, and the sinking feeling now settled like a block of ice in his stomach. The virus was gone. Every copy, every backup. All gone.

10

Rescue

Tom stared at the wall. He knew it was just a representation of the block in his mind, similar to the probability matrix. Representation or not, it still prevented him from accessing any enhanced brain functions. He'd tried to penetrate it through sheer will, forcing the building blocks out of the way, but for everyone he removed, two new ones appeared. Brute force was pointless against this ever-regenerating wall. He needed to tear it down or circumvent it.

It wasn't just the enhanced brain functions of a posthuman he'd lost. He had created complete processing centres in the network that also held research and resulting memories. His own mind had ensured all these were running as separate functions, but they had felt like a part of his mind. He had gone from being a large node cluster to a single imperfect deteriorating node.

He willed himself back to reality. His physical body sat in a comfortable armchair, head lilting to one side, a drop of saliva making its way down his cheek. He'd ingested a large dose of IntelEz hoping to break down the wall, but without success. He wiped the saliva from his cheek and stood up, grabbing hold of the chair as he did so. His senses reported an unfiltered barrage of input. The touch of the clothes against his body, the smell of food and mould from the kitchen, the slight hum from the air-conditioner, the imperfections in the angles of the room. Every minute little detail. Too much for him to deal with.

The mind was an amazing thing, but what it did well was taking shortcuts so it didn't have to process all the data the senses produced. His mind was no longer capable of taking these shortcuts. Every insignificant detail flooded his system. He tried to limit the overload by closing his eyes. He stood in the middle of the room for a few minutes, willing his mind to slow down.

This was the promise of IntelEz. It opened the floodgates of sensory impressions, gave total recall and recalibrated the mind to make sense of it all. People abused the drugs, living in a continuous high of peak intellectual performance. But the brain could only do this for so long. Over years of IntelEz use, it deteriorated, while still barraged with sensory overload.

When he became a posthuman, he was already far down the path towards the half catatonic state of a deadhead. His posthuman mind had nullified this effect, but he suspected he was again susceptible to the deterioration.

This wasn't sustainable. He needed help and the only person left he could ask for a favour had left hours ago and was now probably dead. He opened an encrypted text feed to TikTak.

Tom: I need help.

TikTak: So do I.

Tom: Well, at least you're not dead.

TikTak: No, but I am locked up.

Tom: And they left you network access?

TikTak: No, my Omni implants have basic processing capabilities. I've hacked their surveillance camera in the room to act as a network point. It won't last long.

Tom: I'll come and get you.

TikTak: Really? When I saw you last, you couldn't open a jar of vegemite by yourself.

Tom: I need help. My mind is shutting down. I need help to find who did this.

TikTak: You can't help me. And you can't come here. Leonid is waiting for you.

Tom: I'll think of something. Where are you?

TikTak: Leonid has gone batshit crazy. He killed Elize. He'll kill you too. Don't come!

Tom: What do you want me to do then?

No response. They must have discovered his hack. The news of Elize's death left him untouched. It was as if he could no longer process emotions, or perhaps he just didn't care. There were more pressing concerns. Despite his protests, TikTak needed help. Without posthuman abilities, there was little he could do on his own, but maybe others from his previous life could help. He opened a two-way voice feed to bZane, a low-rent hacker who had helped him out a few times in the past.

"PI man," bZane said. "Didn't think I'd hear from you. You've gone stratospheric!"

"Sorry? What?"

"You can tell me. You're one of the super people, aren't you? Captain Data! Network Man!"

"What are you talking about?"

"I thought you guys were smarter." Tom could hear the disappointment in bZane's voice.

"Can we start again? What are you talking about?"

"We've been tracking you. It is hard not to. Only two other people come close to your online activity profile. Adrian and Elize."

Tom sat back. He was well aware governments and major corporations tracked his activity. As a result, he created a lot of noise to hide what he was actually doing. But he hadn't considered smaller players would have the resources to make any sense of it. Or maybe bZane wasn't the lone hacker he'd imagined.

"Who are we?" he asked.

"Friends," bZane said, and then paused. Tom was just about to ask again when bZane found his voice. "What you guys are doing is crazy!

Couldn't generate traffic like that even with a node army. How do you do it? And why has it stopped?"

Now it was Tom's turn to go silent. bZane's statement confirmed what TikTak had said. Someone was attacking the posthumans, but how and why?

"I need help," Tom said.

"Anything. Another body in the morgue?"

"No. I need to find someone. I'll send you what I have."

Tom sent a collection of id-tags he'd gathered from TikTak over the past few months, hoping at least one of them would provide details of his current location.

"Wow, that's a lot of IDs. Is it a spook?"

"Private contractor."

"Give me a few minutes."

A sound pattern played, disparate sounds merging over time into a voice stating: "You can't handle the truth!" and then dispersing again. The pattern repeated, turning into different quotes each time.

"Got it!" bZane blurted. "I know this guy. He was famous a few years ago. He's gone black ops?"

"Something like it. Can you find him?"

"Yeah, with the IDs you gave me, yes. Just a matter of time."

"Thanks. Let me know when you have something."

"PI man," bZane said just as Tom was about to disconnect.

"Yeah?"

"Why did it stop? We follow patterns on the network. Information flows according to basic algorithms. Easy to predict. The only major disruptors were you guys. Now nothing. Who attacked you?"

"I didn't say anyone attacked us."

"Really? Would you be talking to me now if you weren't? Was it the Chinese?"

"I don't know," Tom said, realising how vulnerable he was in his current state.

"If there is anything we can help with, just let us know."

Again, that strange silence.

"What do you want?" Tom asked.

"Will you tell me how you did it?"

"Did what?" Tom asked, though he knew exactly what she asked about. He needed time to decide how to respond. Was it in his best interest to tell the truth? The probability matrix would have answered that question instantly. Now he found it impossible to draw out the consequences, the cause and effect of any but the most obvious decisions.

"How did you turn into one of them?"

"I didn't," Tom said finally, opting for the truth. "Adrian did it."

"Ok thanks. I'll find him for you."

Just before he disconnected the feed, bZane said, "There is someone else out there. We are not sure at the moment. There are processing centres spread out all over the world. Encryption between them out of this world. A trickle of information flowing between them. We figured it was one of you guys, but if that's not the case, there is someone else."

"A company?"

"We've tried to match the locations to virtual and physical corporate asset registers, but it doesn't align with any legal entity."

"Illegal?"

"Doesn't look like that to us."

"So another posthuman?"

"Maybe. Or someone trying to become one. This happened gradually, calculated. Very different from you guys. You were...messy."

"Thanks. I'll look into it."

bZane disconnected the channel. Tom knew there was more to this conversation. bZane's speech patterns changed enough for him to notice even in his current state. This had been important to bZane, and he hadn't even asked about money. A message appeared on Tom's retina screen: "And this will cost you. Just because you turned into Mr SuperHack doesn't mean I won't charge."

The message comforted him. Perhaps he didn't need to worry about bZane. There had been a lot to their conversation, but he couldn't deal with that now. When he became posthuman, he no longer slept. His brain had partitioned into processing regions, allowing parts to be dormant in a simulated sleep state. But now, both mind and body screamed for rest, for a break from the onslaught of impressions. He couldn't do much anyway until he had located TikTak. He was asleep the second his head hit the pillow.

Tom woke up just before the incoming feed notification. Some of his posthuman capabilities were still operational, even if he couldn't access them. It stood to reason. He'd enhanced his nervous system and other functions of his body. They would have failed by now without posthuman capabilities operating them. There was hope after all, he thought as he connected to the feed.

"Information processing Boy!"

Tom winced. He wished bZane would settle on a name. "Yes?"

"I found him! And I can help you get him out!"

"How?"

"This is TikTak remember? I just opened the door."

***

TikTak sat in the small examination room, assessing his options. Leonid was suffering from some kind of breakdown. His actions were erratic, driven by emotion with no clear direction. He'd seen what awaited Tom if he sided with Leonid. It was likely he would share Tom's fate once Leonid captured him. He had to find a way out of this without a deal. He'd already checked the room for escape routes. The surveillance camera ran an old firmware and he'd been able to hack it through the low-level protocols, but the adaptive security agents on the network discovered him in less than a minute. They also rectified the firmware. Now he had no network access at all.

CLICK!

TikTak turned to the door, waiting for someone to enter. Seconds passed, but it remained unopened. He tried the doorhandle. It was unlocked. His first instinct was to leave it be, thinking it was some kind of trick. Decker would stand on the other side of the door, waiting for him to escape. That was a good enough excuse for an accidental death.

A message blinked on his Omni-lens.

"Go!" it said. "They are coming for you!"

It took him completely by surprise. The security agents removed his surveillance camera hack. Decker had taken his Omni, and he'd assumed it was out of range for his implants. So how could there be a message? It wasn't Decker's style. He was much more direct in his approach. The thought provided little comfort, but enough for TikTak to go with his gut.

He opened the door and ran down the corridor. He only had a vague idea of which direction to go and hoped his mysterious helper would provide guidance, but no such luck. There were no further messages. He needed to reach the upper levels, but as he turned a corner, he saw a mercenary standing with his back towards him. He stopped and retreated behind the corner, trying to remember another way out. If he engaged anyone in battle, they'd just swarm the place, so he had to remain unseen. He headed back the way he came. When he came close to the examination room, another message appeared.

"Your Omni is close. I've activated it. There are intermittent connections. Find it and I can help."

"Who are you?" TikTak sent in reply.

"Tom sends his regards," the response came.

TikTak smiled. There was still hope. First things first, he needed his Omni. He wouldn't be able to escape without it. It didn't have a long range, only two metres for a consistent high-speed connection, so it had to be close. It was not in the examination room. Nearby rooms seemed equally unlikely, especially after walking a few steps away from his current position. It had to be on the floor above. Crouching down confirmed this as he lost contact with his Omni when he tried it.

Each floor was a circle with rooms fanning out from the centre. The middle section contained bathrooms, storage and two central staircases. With luck, the way to the second staircase would be clear. He started down the corridor again, this time in the opposite direction. He made it to the stairwell and to the floor above without incident. It was early in the morning, so he wasn't expecting anyone here. The floor he entered was usually busy, and the cover of the crowd would have been useful. He had a quick look through the door. It was empty.

He decided speed was more important than caution and ran to the room above his cell. He opened the door and saw Decker sit at a table in a small conference room. On the table lay Tiktak's Omni and baton.

"Your Omni activated again," Decker said with a grin. "Figured you'd be close behind."

"Give it to me."

Decker shook his head. "You want it? Come and get it."

TikTak studied his opponent. Decker was unarmed from what he could tell and remained sitting. He even leant back in the chair as if he had nothing to worry about. It was almost like he wanted TikTak to make the first move from a position of strength.

"Really? Scared? How about this?"

Decker threw the telescopic baton on the ground in front of TikTak. He picked it up, weighed it in his hands and flicked it open to full length. He couldn't see anything wrong with it.

"So let's go."

Decker shifted his weight to get out of the chair. TikTak figured he wouldn't get a better opportunity, so he struck aiming for his head.

It didn't connect. Instead of standing up, Decker remained low in a kneeling stance and blocked the strike with his underarm.

"Won't be that easy," Decker said.

"You have armour implants?"

He nodded. "Nothing you can tamper with. I've seen you hack augmentations. These are passive. Nothing to hack."

TikTak struck again, but Decker blocked it as he stood up. He launched into a flurry of strikes, making sure each of them varied in height and angle, but Decker blocked them with ease. TikTak took a step back and studied his opponent. He had trained with Decker many times and knew he was a decent ground fighter and only passable boxer. He shouldn't have been able to block all those strikes. It was almost as if he knew where the next strike would land. Mind reading tech had come a long way, but this was impossible.

Decker smiled. "Is that all you've got?"

TikTak's Omni was close enough now for a stable connection, so he sent off a question to whoever had contacted him before.

"I need help. Can you hack my opponent?"

"Let me see," the reply came back.

Decker attacked with sledgehammer-like blows. They weren't hard to block, but every strike shook his defences. TikTak had expected him to go for his legs and take him down to the ground, but he wasn't even trying to position himself for that. Decker seemed content to just pound his defences until there was nothing left.

"There is nothing to hack," the reply came back. "He's amped up if that helps."

TikTak nodded to himself. That was it. IntelEz increased your awareness and ability to process visual input. If you added another drug that enhanced focus, you'd be able to predict what your opponent would do.

"You needed to amp up to fight me," he told Decker. "I'm flattered."

Decker struck again. TikTak held his baton at both ends, using it to block the blow and immediately let go of one side, sweeping it down towards Decker's legs. It wasn't a powerful strike, but it was fast. Decker moved back quick enough for the baton to just glance off his leg, but it was enough to give him pause for thought.

"Didn't expect that," TikTak said with a grin.

Decker took a step forward. TikTak responded with a strike towards his head as a reflex action. Decker blocked the blow and grabbed the baton before TikTak could pull it back.

"Didn't expect that," Decker mimicked.

TikTak pulled the baton and struck Decker in the face with his left fist over and over. Decker let go of the baton, grabbed TikTak's arm and swept his legs. TikTak realised this was what Decker had been waiting for. No matter what you do to change yourself with augmentation and surgery, you still fought to your strengths. Decker preferred ground fighting.

TikTak landed on his side and tried to roll back, but Decker held on to his left arm.

He had to free himself. If Decker got the advantage on the ground, this fight would be over. He still had the baton in his right hand and swung at Decker's head, who just grabbed it and pinned TikTak down by resting one of his knees on TikTak's chest.

"Not so cocky anymore," Decker said as he wrenched the baton from TikTak's grip.

The door flew open, but TikTak couldn't see who it was from his position.

"You killed her! You killed all of her!"

As Decker looked up towards this new threat, he loosened his grip a little, allowing TikTak to turn around enough to see the new intruder. Dr Menker stood in the door opening with a shock gun aimed at Decker.

"Hey, now, hold…" Decker started. Dr Menker fired the gun. The air fizzled as the electric payload passed close to Decker's head. He let go of TikTak and backed away.

"Just hold on here. Let's talk about this."

"There is nothing to talk about!" Dr Menker said and fired again.

TikTak grabbed his Omni and ran. He saw no other mercenaries on his way out of the building.

TikTak took the first Rent-a-cab that responded, trying to make sense of what had happened. Could all this still be Adrian? He remembered the video files and watched the next one. As he did, he received an encrypted message from Tom.

"Meet me where we first met."

11

Adrian's Video Clip #2

The image flickered to life again, a complete black that gained texture and shape. It was a close-up of the iris of an eye, filling the entire field of vision and then pulled back to show the middle-aged man staring right at the camera. Behind him sat people in rows, all dressed the same. He looked up, addressing the gathered people behind the camera. He shook his head and grimaced as if in pain.

"My children!" He started. "Hopefully you are still with me and share my passion for humanity, but I need you to understand a few things before I go on."

He sat down on the floor cross-legged.

"The evolution of humanity has reached a dead end. Self-awareness and all it entails is an evolutionary experiment gone awry. Our development may self-adjust. I don't know. What I know is that you are doomed as a species. There is no other way to put it. Humankind as we know it will not survive much longer. You can hide behind your collective ignorance, but it won't change reality. As long as individual rights and needs are absolutes, humankind will kill itself. Once we've depleted or poisoned our natural resources, we will descend into war over what remains."

The middle-aged man slumped where he sat, as if spent. A heavy-set girl, maybe twelve years old, stood up from the rows of people behind him.

"That unit is depleted," she said. "Its brain functions no longer able to hold the focal point of my mind." Her voice, matched with Adrian's intonation, sounded like a schoolmistress in the making.

The child looked down on itself, studying its form disapprovingly. "This will have to do."

The middle-aged man was dragged off-screen, while the girl placed herself in the same position where he'd been. The camera operator adjusted the angle to match her height.

"Can you change?" she asked. "No, that isn't possible. These behaviours are so ingrained into you. History has shown repeatedly that, given limited resources, we die or leave the location. The Easter Island inhabitants, the Mayan civilization, the kingdom of Mesopotamia, the list goes on and on."

She stood up, fixed her stare at the camera. It was obvious this performance was for the video, not the gathered people.

"But what do you do when that location is the world? Maintaining equilibrium was never a strong human trait. You, even more so than most living things, are good at one thing and one thing only. Expansion. That's why you look up at the sky, imagining new worlds. That's why you stare into your microscopes, imagining smaller and smaller particles. But when there is nowhere else to go, you create artificial expansion by taking from each other. You come up with ideas such as free trade agreements and market economy, but it is just another name for the same thing. The pursuit of expansion."

She shook her head and stood for a while, head bowed.

"I am not the answer to this problem either," she said and then looked at them almost defiantly. "I thought I was. Hell, I knew I was! But I am flawed just like you. Even worse! I could change, but I didn't. I took your brothers and sisters and turned them into hardware for my ever-expanding mind. Again, expansion. How does that differ from a multinational corporation taking over smaller businesses?"

She returned her attention to the camera, fixing it with a stare. "We need to be defined by something else. We need to hack humankind.

And it needs to be a big hack that will last over generations. A hack that will redefine who you are, with me as the guide. But this is easy to say. An artificial start to a new form of intelligence isn't likely to bring a positive result. There are countless parameters when creating intelligence. Instant macroevolution removes the most important one—time to adapt."

She went quiet, letting this sink in. "External parameters forces immediate reactions, and they are almost always hostile. It becomes a revolution, and however much we'd like to think this is a good thing, it never is. Actual change happens in degrees over a long time."

She smiled and held out her hands as if to encompass something unseen. "Humankind 2.0. What could that be? And do I even have the mental faculties to work that out?"

12

Virus Fulfilled

Megan left the Omniscient Networks Headquarters. Her first instinct was to go to one of her current overnight suites. Six hotels had rooms prepared for her specific requirements, but they billed to the company and her entry would be recorded. They'd pick her up within the hour if she went to any of those. It was time for contingency plans.

Ever since the board of directors discovered her secret and decided not to report her to the police, she knew a time would come when she'd need to disappear. With enough money, it was possible to buy anything from new identities to silence, but in this connected world hiding the trail of such dealings was almost impossible. She needed the boundaries only geography and politics provided.

Her first thought was one of the southern states. The US split into two factions, the North and the South. A recent president created a rift between the two major parties which caused a constitutional crisis. A few of the states decided not to join either, feeling they were better off on their own, such as California, and formed the Independent States of America. The split crippled US as a force on the international stage and cross-border cooperation was tentative. But her company was prevalent throughout all the states. She needed to go further.

China hadn't allowed IntelEz into the general population. Illegal imports still occurred, but their workforce was relatively unaffected. There were massive layoffs as the demand for products had taken a nosedive, but at least their workforce wasn't a societal liability like the deadheads in most other countries.

She'd set up a safe house in Hong Kong, deeming it the easiest location for her and other westerners to visit. But she hadn't expected events to escalate with such speed. Her counterfeit documentation remained in one of her overnight suites. She needed to retrieve it. Sree would have them all watched as soon as he discovered what she'd done.

She entered the hotel knowing full well at least half a dozen systems already logged her and her identity tag, but she didn't have a choice. The elevator wouldn't even take her to her floor if it failed to scan her tag. Automation and security came at a price and she'd been the first to agree it was worth it.

A warning flickered across her vision as she stood in the elevator, alerting her someone tried to access the backup copies of the virus. Sree knew what she'd done, and he'd come after her full force. He had to. Without her, he was finished.

The elevator door opened directly into the suite. She headed for the kitchen, opened the oven and pulled out the envelope. Another warning flickered, this time more urgent. She had created a watch list of anyone associated with Omniscient Networks or any of its subsidiaries and four of them now triggered her perimeter alarm. They were employees of a small expert security firm, and here to secure her as soon as possible. Sree would be close behind with more men. However much she thought she'd prepared for this event, it wasn't enough. In reality, she never expected it to come to this, so it had been more of a token gesture. Setting up the safe houses, get the documentation, it was all just throwing money around. Needing a proper escape plan from each of the overnight suites never seemed important. Not until now.

She opened the envelope and smiled. At least she'd prepared a way to fight back. The Omniscient Networks would be the first to claim they'd never misuse the network or the devices, but they still explored options to ensure they were ready if someone else did. The Drainer was an example of this. An integrated Omni and other enhancements drew part of their power from the body itself. The Drainer removed any fail-safes and increased the energy pulled from the body hundredfold. The envelope contained a memTag with override codes to trigger that function.

A private elevator to her suite seemed a great idea, but as she ran towards it and saw the blinking arrow, she swore to herself. There had to be another way out, a fire escape somewhere. But she was on the fiftieth floor. She refused to run down fifty flights of stair just to be caught at the bottom. Instead, she loaded the memTag codes on her Omni, hid the envelope under her clothes and stood by the elevator waiting.

When it opened, two men entered the apartment. They were from the private security firm the company used for high-profile visitor. They were nothing more than glorified bodyguards, but they'd still sport enhancements. Their suits were tailored to hide them, but it was easy enough to see if you knew what to look for. Augmentations caused a small shift in the centre of gravity, affecting movement ever so slightly. In fact, she counted on it. The Drainer would work much better if they did. They had integrated Omnis, but that wouldn't be enough.

Now all she needed was their Omni tags to direct the attack. This proved easier than expected. One of them had a public id that flashed as soon as she looked at him.

"Megan Barrelle?"

"You know who I am."

"The board has requested you attend their meeting."

"They have a meeting now? At 4am?"

"Please come with us."

"And who are you?"

"What?"

"I'm Megan. We've established that. Your friend here is Mark Miller, and he has a smiley as his middle name. I didn't realise you could do that?"

"Sure can," Mark said with a cocky smile.

"I know his name," she continued, "because he's an Omni tag slut leaving it out there for anyone to grab. But who are you?"

He looked at Mark who just shrugged in return.

"I'm not going anywhere until I know who you are."

"Fine," he said and an Omni-greet appeared seconds later. He turned to Mark, "And I told you it isn't normal to have your Omni tag on broadcast."

"Works for me."

"It is like you are walking around with a billboard with a big arrow on it."

"Works for me," he repeated.

"Unprofessional is what it is."

While they argued, Megan researched the two id tags enough to know they both had integrated Omnis and basic enhancements. Nothing beyond a basic package, but she thought it would be enough.

"The board is waiting?" she said to them and entered the elevator. They followed her.

As soon as the door closed, she activated the drainer-protocol and waited. Her two captors kept arguing, and it turned increasingly personal.

When the doors opened, Mark had to lean against the wall not to fall over.

"Fuck you both," she said as she left the elevator, leaving the two behind.

Mark reached out towards her, but she easily slapped his arm aside. On the way out of the hotel, she swapped her Omni tag to a fake id and jumped into a Rent-a-cab and ordered it to take her to the airport. The board could put her on every intelligence agency watch list if they wanted to, and they probably would. She had to get out of the country before that happened. She didn't dare to use one of the corporate jets. Instead, she booked the first available flight to Hong Kong using the same fake identity she used for the Rent-a-cab. She also booked ten other flights to different parts of the world at the same time.

She knew it wouldn't make much difference, but she still applied the face-sculpting salve. It wouldn't pass a biometric scan, but it changed your features enough to fool facial recognition algorithms most of the time. She felt the muscles tensing in response to the salve.

The airport was dead. People travelled less now, while the sizeable buildings remained. IntelEz was the main reason, but virtual alternatives were also available. Business meetings were held in neuro-space now. As a result, the big jumbo jets of the past were replaced with Faster-Than-Sound jets that took fewer passengers but provided more comfort and faster travel.

She walked through the VIP lane, feeling very exposed. Escaping the country had never seemed real to her. As a result, her preparations were less than perfect. She had a fake passport, but it would only function if she also hacked the airport systems to match the bio-prints. That required preparation, and a hack applied just before she used the passport. Instead, she travelled as herself and cloned the entry over and over as if she was going to multiple destinations at the same time. That was much easier for her to do on her own.

The only thing in her favour was speed, and as she waited for the biometrics scan, it didn't feel adequate at all. She didn't think they'd have a board meeting now, but it would definitely be today and once that happened, all bets were off.

The bio-scan finished, and the passport control system allowed her through. She turned off her Omni to prevent leaving any digital prints that would give away her actual destination. The giant corridors leading to the planes were desolate, her footsteps echoing as she half-ran through the middle, using travelators where available. She had to get out of here, and somehow she'd convinced herself the plane was a safe place. If she could just get there, she'd be ok.

"Please turn on your Omni to be guided to your seat," a voice said before she entered the plane.

"It is malfunctioning. I will find my seat."

"Make manual selections once you get to your seat."

"I will."

Everything was hooked to the Omnis, and it allowed automation to replace most service roles. In a way, her company had counteracted the loss in the workforce from people turning into deadheads.

The plane only took a hundred passengers, so finding the seat was easy enough. She counted ten other people on the flight. The face-sculpting salve should be enough to remain unrecognised. She'd been out of the public eye the past year, but people still recognised her wherever she went.

She waited for the plane to take off. Hong Kong wasn't her ideal destination, but with one advantage. Omniscient Networks hadn't been able to crack the Chinese market. A government backed company released a suspected reverse engineered localised copy called Cangjie. It had connected so much better with the Asian market, the Omniscient Networks no longer had a presence there. While she had ranted about the intellectual theft at length to the Chinese ambassador on many previous occasions, now she was happy about it.

She swapped the id-tag in her Omni and planted false trails with the other tickets she had purchased, checking them all in and booked transport and hotels on the other side. She did the same for Hong Kong, ensuring it wouldn't stand out from the others.

It wasn't until the plane was in the air that she finally relaxed. Her shoulders ached as the tension released.

The wait in Hong Kong customs reignited her concerns. Was she on a global watch list? They could if they wanted to, but perhaps the board still regarded her as an asset and not just a liability. Either way, she had to watch her back. Her face itched as the face-sculpting salve wore off. The last thing she wanted was to leave facial prints to be discovered later. She'd ensure the airline tracking of her arriving in each of the booked destinations would be there, but if they found another corroborating trail in any of those locations, they'd be able to tell the false trails from the real one.

She walked through the bio-print scanner and waited for a second as it matched her bio-print with the one in her passport. After an all-clear, she hurried through the airport and onto the MTR, and even though she opted for anonymous payment methods, she ensured to stay out of cameras whenever she could. People crowded around her as the door to the train opened and it reminded her of how much she hated Hong Kong. There were just too many people here.

She took a deep breath of relief for the first in a long time. Maybe there were too many people here, but none of them cared about her. She was free from prying eyes and pointless demands, free to focus on what she wanted. For the first time since the board removed her from her post as CIO, she was her own agent.

She stepped out from Kwun Tong MTR station and pulled the hoodie over her head. The street was busy. A world of neon holograms, food stalls and small stands selling anything and everything. She ignored the visual overload, but the smell from the food stalls along the road was something else entirely. When had she eaten last? A look at the airplane food had been enough to remain fasting through the flight. She raided the food stalls, buying an assortment of street food, from fish balls to deep-fried tofu, digging through the bags for something to eat as she walked. Her destination wasn't far from here.

Kwun Tong had been a major industrial area, but as the factories moved to mainland China, many of the warehouses and buildings were demolished to make way for residential buildings. She bought one of these old buildings and left it abandoned for the past year. She'd sent in a cleaning crew, but as she opened it for the first time, she realised they'd not finished the job. The main hall, the size of a small hangar, was empty apart from stacks of e-pallets and empty crates. They'd removed machinery and shelves, but the floor was littered with bolts and shrapnel.

She tried to ignore it. She'd spent too much time in the meat-space, with the messiness and physical restrictions of the biological world, where most time was spent on pointless pursuits, driven by base needs.

The logical world had no such restrictions. She longed for the day when she could download herself into the network. When she ran the company, she diverted a sizeable portion of the research budget to that specific area. She estimated that the first prototypes were five years away with proper funding.

It was with a sigh of relief she hooked up to the local network. She assessed the reserved network allocation and increased it a hundredfold. The companies owning the warehouse and the computing resources were not connected to her, but to be on the safe side, she increased the level of encryption of data both in transmission and rest. The resulting loss of speed couldn't be helped.

She loaded the virus into the network partition and watched it grow until it used up all available network resources. She located the nexus node and fed it a text file with the full DNA sequence of the German cockroach. The effect rippled through the network, reprogramming nodes through partial replication. In less than an hour, the entire network was alight with communication. She watched the communication load, mesmerised by how different parts of the network organised itself. But into what? If her suspicion was right, it needed external input.

She fought the instinctual behaviour to contact someone for help. This went beyond her understanding and she needed expert input. Was this, as she suspected, a simulation of a living organism, or was it only the nervous system? Or something else entirely?

She was used to delegating any task in her life she either didn't want to or couldn't do to others. To remain undetected, she'd have to keep a low online profile, else a Behavioural Pattern Analyser would locate her. Online activity left a unique pattern, much like a fingerprint on a crime scene. The less she was online, the better.

She rifled through the plastic bags for more to eat. She found grilled tofu in a box and devoured the content. It was already cold, but she hardly noticed. She sat back, fascinated by the mystery. She yawned. However tantalising this problem was, the biological imperative of sleep demanded its due. Some theorised that the posthumans could partition their sleep to allow parts of their mind to remain active. She envied them that capability. That was another area where she spent a lot of the research budget. How to turn someone posthuman. She'd even spent some on just limiting sleep. Neither had led anywhere.

She rested despite her inner voice demanding she continue until she solved the problem.

Four hours later, she woke up and headed for the golden arcade at Sham Shui Poo to purchase additional parts. On the way, she bought Macanese pork chop buns and two egg tarts and ate as she traversed the city on the MTR and on foot. She knew facial recognition systems were almost impossible to escape here, but she had no choice.

She entered the maze of little stores, pushing her way through the crowd. Each stand brimmed with a mixture of old and new tech, some specialised, but most offered a wide variety of gadgets. She didn't want to be there at all, but she steeled herself and pushed onwards past the first row of stands into the heart of the arcade. She stopped at a high-tech toy stand and negotiated a price for a small remote-controlled drone with a camera and paid with weCoins, one of the more popular anonymous digital currencies.

Back at the warehouse, she reprogrammed the drone and fed the video and gyroscope into the nexus node, while connecting the remote controls to other nodes. It was mostly guesswork, but hoped it would work nonetheless. She stared at it for ten minutes. Nothing happened.

She studied the node map, but apart from processing the input from the video feed, there was no evidence it was leading anywhere. Why had she expected this to be the case? Maybe what she was seeing was just a simulation. She was just about to shut the drone off when a rotor twitched. It started and stopped repeatedly, each time running for a few seconds longer. Then it reversed and spun backwards. It was testing the rotors one by one.

A day later, it rose a few centimetres from the ground for the first time and dropped back down. This pattern repeated, with minor adjustments each time. She unplugged it from its charging station once it rose high enough to strain against the cable. The communication within the node-cluster lit up like a Christmas tree. She had no way to decipher what it meant, but it was the direct result of learning to operate the drone and processing its visual feed.

It spun, taking in its surroundings. When Megan came into view, it hovered for a long time and slowly approached her. She held up her hand in a greeting, causing the drone to fly back into the wall, damaging its rotors. It dropped to the floor, ended up on its side and spun ineffectively. It stopped and tested its rotors, finding the damaged one. Compensating with the other rotors, it rose again from the ground just as the batteries ran out.

Megan sat and stared at the drone. It was intelligent, maybe even self-aware. No other conclusion made sense. She'd worked with different machine learning methods, but this was beyond anything she'd ever seen. It had learnt to control the drone in a day without knowing the interface. That in itself was a technological marvel. Creating problem solving algorithms in pursuing general artificial intelligence was nothing new, but it required boundaries and preset goals to function.

To begin with, you needed a purpose, something to achieve. But you also needed the drive to pursue it and an understanding of the tools it had to achieve them. This, whatever it was, had none of that. Maybe the goal was just survival, but how could that translate into learning to process a visual feed and the controls of a drone? There was something else here. Curiosity perhaps?

Whatever this was, she was sure of one thing. This was her ticket back to control of her company again.

13

Past Sins

The day after Megan's escape, Sree entered the boardroom on the top floor of the Omniscient Networks headquarter. Three executives sat at the table already, hooked into the neural feed. Why they even bothered with boardrooms was beyond him. People could jack in wherever they wanted. But to be seen and interact in real life was still the best way to do business. If you could be bothered to meet someone in person, they were important to you.

Two-way neural interfaces were still very much a luxury. He wouldn't have been able to afford one, but his job role required it, so he'd been fitted with one at the corporates expense. If his contract ended, he'd have a hefty bill to pay back. He paused for a second before jacking in. This was it. The outcome of this meeting could very well define his future in the industry. He took a deep breath and connected to the neuro-feed.

He ended up in a waiting room, a mid-western plain stretching as far as the eye could see. It was supposed to be calming, but the desolation gave no distraction from his racing mind. He transitioned from desperate hope to guaranteed doom in the space of a heartbeat.

A door opened out of nowhere. This was his cue. He was being summoned to the meeting. The location he entered was a replica of the boardroom his physical body was in. While he understood the reason for this, it was still disappointing. The board members sat around the table, studying him. They too were accurate representations of their physical bodies, minus any imperfections.

"Now we have the matter of our wayward founder," Lars Sorensen, CEO, said. "What's the status?"

Sree had never met Lars in the physical world. In neuro-space he was the archetypal Scandinavian. Blond, blue eyes with high cheekbones and a stare that reflected the coldness of his country of origin.

"She disappeared while committing corporate theft," Alex Rind said. "The stolen software is potentially dangerous and almost definitely of posthuman origins."

"And you are here why?" He asked and looked straight at Sree. The menacing stare from his neuro-avatar had him fumble for words.

"He's here because he lost her," Alex said.

"I see. And do you know where she is?"

"No," Sree started.

"She left the country," Alex interrupted.

"We don't know that," Sree said and immediately regretted it.

"She left the country," Alex repeated, slower this time.

"And how can you be of help?"

Sree looked over at Alex, expecting him to answer, but Alex nodded for him to respond.

"I know how she behaves, her patterns. Give me a week, and she'll be back here."

"You have two days," Lars said in a tone that did not invite discussion. "I don't think there is any reason to protect her any longer. Let's release what we have on her."

"I would advise against that," Sree said. "If we want the virus back, we have to get to her first."

"We only have anecdotal information about her whereabouts. Mainly from you. We will release the information. If you can't find her, maybe local law enforcement can."

Sree nodded.

"And if you have nothing to report in two days, consider it one failure too many."

"I have reservations about bringing in law enforcement," Alex started, but Sree's neuro-link disconnected before he could hear anything more. He faded back to the boardroom, sitting in the same spot as he had in the neuro-simulation.

Two days! It would take him longer than that to trace all the different locations Megan had pretended to travel to. He suspected she was still in the country and had many behavioural pattern agents running trying to find her, but without luck so far. He looked out over the skyline, collecting his thoughts. Dark clouds were gathering in the distance, obscuring the rising sun. A storm was on its way. He found it fitting the weather reflected his current situation.

What would Megan do? He could only think of two driving forces behind her next steps. She would want to keep investigating the virus. Once she had her sight on something, she didn't let go. Ever. The other was revenge. She was a spiteful bitch at the best of times and held grudges for years. She would want to hurt the board members who held her ransom and him for turning her in.

Alex sighed, interrupting his thoughts.

"That went better than expected," Alex said, as he rubbed his temples. "I get a headache from the new neuro-software. I'm hoping they'll sort it out."

"Better? I have two days, or I'm out of a job."

"I thought they'd fire you on the spot. Believe me. Better."

"Are they still going to release what we have on her?"

"Yeah. No luck there. It will be out before the end of the day."

Sree doubted it would make a difference.

bZane to the Rescue

The car stopped, waiting for TikTak to accept the completion of the journey. He had booked it with a clean id-tag, hoping it would delay any pursuers. It was unlikely to fool them for long.

The small playground sandwiched between the two houses hadn't changed. It felt like a lifetime ago, but it had only been twelve months since they'd met here for the first time. Tom was already there. He was wandering back and forth in the small space between the swings and a climbing net. He had not yet seen TikTak.

"Hey there, Rainbow shitting Unicorn!" TikTak yelled.

Tom smiled.

"We need to go," TikTak continued. "Leonid's men will be here soon."

"What happened?"

"Leonid has gone batshit crazy. Had Elize killed in front of me."

"And the rest of her?"

"Don't know, but Leonid ordered them all killed."

"Wait," Tom said and held up his hand. "Someone has a lock on your position."

"bZane helping you out?"

Tom nodded.

"Can't afford better?"

"I like him. He helped you to get out."

"Really? That was bZane?"

Tom nodded.

"So not useless then."

A car pulled up, and the door opened as they approached.

"Where to now?" Sam asked.

TikTak looked at his friend and shrugged his shoulders. "No idea."

Sam ordered the car to drive towards the city centre.

"Someone targeted the posthumans. When we were taking care of Adrian's final nodes, you were both attacked. Whoever planned this knew where Elize was and could get to her and also knew you'd be attacking the safe house with me."

"Leonid?"

"Not before today, I think. You and Elize were helping him."

"Yes, but once the threat of Adrian was gone…"

"No. Attacking Elize, not knowing if it would kill his granddaughter? It just doesn't sound like him."

"Then who?"

"I watched the video clips from Adrian. He wants to hack humanity, whatever that means. Maybe he needed you and Elize gone for that to happen?"

"Sounds as good as any theory. So we still have a rogue Adrian to deal with?" Tom fell silent for a moment. "That matches something bZane told me. He's noticed someone else building a node army. Someone still active."

"So another Adrian cluster?"

"Or something part of his plan."

"Did you bring the memTag I gave you? The one from the silo?"

Tom nodded and handed him an envelope.

"Maybe this will give us something."

TikTak inserted the memTag into an isolated Omni reader. Together with the video files, it contained one executable file. He isolated it from any network communication before triggering it.

"What is it?" Tom asked.

"Hang on. It is prompting for video. I'll stream it to my Omni-lens."

A lo-res VR model of Adrian's face appeared in front of him.

"What's the password?" it said with a grin.

"Adrian is a loser?" TikTak entered.

"No, no, no," the face said, a finger appearing, wagging back and forth. "No, no, no. Try again if you dare, Tann."

He stopped. The password agent had mentioned him by name. His legal, almost forgotten name. That seemed a strange thing to program into a password agent.

"Who are you?" he entered.

"I'm the gatekeeper. What's the password?"

Gatekeeper? TikTak ran a search, getting hits on an old classic pre-neural movie. It suggested Key Master, Zulu, and Gozer.

The password agent dismissed them all.

"Not so easy, Tann. Try again."

TikTak swore to himself and disconnected.

"What is it?" Tom repeated.

TikTak disconnected the agent.

"Another of Adrian's stupid mind games. He's protected the content with a password agent."

"So what now?"

"Hang on."

TikTak ran a check on the security perimeter of their safe house. No alarms had triggered, but he hadn't expected that. Leonid and his mercenaries would have tripped them for sure, but there was someone else behind this. Whether this someone would trigger the alarms or just set up his own perimeter was impossible to know.

"I checked the safe house. It seems ok, but I'm not sure if that's enough."

"We'll have to take the chance. We don't have any other options right now."

Tom nodded.

TikTak sat back and pulled up the final video file from the memTag in the hope it would bring clarity. He was just about to watch it when a truck ran into them from the side.

***

Tom saw the oncoming truck and felt their vehicle speed up to evade it. As a result, the truck hit their car at the rear, sending it spinning along the road.

Tom felt surprisingly calm as he braced himself for whatever was to come. It was as if he was stationary, with the world spinning around his axis instead of the other way around. The Assisted Driver Network adjusted the surrounding traffic, giving their vehicle room to recover, but they could still head into oncoming traffic if it wasn't fast enough. Or even worse, there could be a human driver incapable of dealing with the situation. He had no way of telling. The car still spun too fast for him to focus on the world outside. There was no way for him to control the outcome, so he had to trust fate to be kind. Or maybe he just didn't care anymore.

The world stopped spinning as their vehicle came to a halt in the middle of the highway. The truck backed up, like a plane readying itself to career down the runway.

"We need to get out of here," Tom said and looked over at TikTak. His friend didn't respond. He was slumped over, held in place by the seatbelt. Blood dripped from a cut on the side of his head.

"I've charged the ride to your account," the car said. "Have a good day."

Tom swore. The truck headed towards them yet again, slow at first but picking up speed. He shoved his shoulder against the door next to him repeatedly, but it was jammed shut. He climbed over TikTak, undid his seatbelt, and tried the opposite door. It protested, but opened up enough for him to squeeze through. The oncoming truck had finished half the distance between them. He was just about to pull TikTak out.

"What..." TikTak looked around, dazed.

"Get out! Now!"

To TikTak's credit, he immediately pulled himself out of the wreckage unassisted. As soon as he cleared the vehicle, Tom grabbed him and dragged him away from the car just before the truck hit it, sending it flying down the road.

"Move!" Tom yelled and pulled the still dazed TikTak along with him off the street. The truck backed up again, trying to align itself with their escape path.

"What happened?" TikTak looked around and saw the truck. "Shit! We need to get off the road!"

Their car had spun into a protected induction road. It allowed cars to charge while they were driving. This was bad news. The road stretched for kilometres and had high fences on both sides to protect anyone from walking into the electrical field.

"We can't!" Tom considered climbing the fence, but knew they'd be easy targets. The only way out was past the truck. Running in a straight line down a highway with a homicidal vehicle behind them wasn't an option.

TikTak just stood there, mesmerised by the truck that now had reversed far enough to align itself with their position. He walked backwards, still staring at it.

"We can't go that way," Tom said to TikTak, who still didn't respond. "Maybe if we split up and run to either side, we may confuse it," Tom suggested, realising immediately what a bad a plan that was. This was a machine with a singular purpose. It was just going to make a split-second decision to mow one of them down as a partially achieved goal and then go for the other.

The truck was a 50-tonne black monstrosity. In Tom's mind, its engines revved, even though it was silent as its electric motors propelled it towards them.

"Stay where you are," TikTak said. "Just do as I say."

The truck approached, faster and faster. When it was fifteen metres away from them, it swerved to the side, going through the fence and ploughing into a building. The momentum kept it moving towards them, side first, threatening to topple over. Two meters away, it leaned precariously before falling back again onto its wheels.

"Now we go," TikTak said. "More hacked cars will come."

They made their way through the gaping hole in the fence. Adrenaline pumped through his system. He didn't want to die, at least that much was clear. He may no longer be a posthuman, but if Leonid thought Tom would be an easy target, he'd prove him wrong.

"How do they track us?" Tom said as he climbed over remnants of the composite fence.

"They've been following me all along," TikTak replied. "They let me out. That was why it was so easy for bZane to free me. I should have seen it. They couldn't care less about me. They want you dead. We need to get off the grid long enough to lose them."

A blue Rent-a-cab approached them, and the window opened halfway. A girl, about twenty years old, with multi-coloured dreadlocks framing her face, sat in the cab waving at them frenetically.

"Doctor Wi-Fi! TikTak! You need to drop your Omnis. That is how they know where you are!"

TikTak threw his Omni as far as he could.

"Who are you?" Tom asked.

"I'm bZane," she said. "And yes, I'm not what you expected."

"She's with them," TikTak said. "She will take us straight to them."

"Really?" she said. "The gang who tried to squash you with a truck would send me in a cab? Brilliant plan."

"You're the backup plan."

"You can be pizza on the road for all I care. I'm here for Tom. He's my client."

Tom listened to them arguing. It was true he hadn't expected bZane to be so young, or a girl. He'd been working with bZane on and off for the last five years.

"What was the first thing I asked you to do?" Tom asked her.

"Hack your daughter's school records."

Tom smiled. This was indeed the first task he had given bZane as a test.

"Doesn't matter," TikTak said. "We can't trust her."

"I do," Tom said, dropped his Omni on the ground and opened the car door, motioning for TikTak to enter. "But why did you pretend to be a guy?"

"Not now! We need to go!"

TikTak shrugged and entered the car.

***

Rent-a-cabs usually had two sets of seats facing each other, like a small limousine, since it no longer needed front seats facing the road. This meant TikTak was now facing the girl. He stared at her and she stared back, challenging him to say anything. She was short, not more than a meter and a half, dressed in camouflage pants and an oversized hoodie. Her irises shone as if they were backlit. It could be just cosmetic, but he guessed this was in line with other enhancements. She looked like the antithesis of a government or corporate agent, but they came in all sized nowadays.

"They will find us," he said. "I can guarantee they are already tracking this car."

She shook her head. "Don't worry. I've got this covered."

The car drove off and soon entered a tunnel. Halfway through, the car stopped and bZane instructed them to get out. It continued its journey, while they walked through a service tunnel and a set of stairs to another road, where a car was waiting for them.

"They'll just match our travel patterns with this car," TikTak said.

She shook her head. "Not according to the control system. It is on the way to pick someone up, so there's no one in the car. That's the way we get around. We hack cars to pick us up when they are on their way somewhere else. There is always an empty Rent-a-cab on its way somewhere."

"What about the cameras in here?"

"On most models they don't operate when the cab is empty. But we can turn them off if we have to."

"Yeah, ok," he said. He had to admit it was clever. Their travel, as long as they didn't have their Omnis, would be impossible to track.

"You can have my old Omnis," she said and dumped a chunky bracelet next to TikTak and an old-fashioned Omni with a screen next to Tom. "Sorry, they're old, but at least they're clean."

Tom had mentioned bZane before, so he knew a bit about her. Before he joined EvoII as an operative, he'd been a hacker for hire himself. It took a certain kind of person to survive in that game. She didn't look the part.

TikTak studied the bracelet. It was only a generation old. He saw she was wearing the most current version of the bracelet right now.

"Where are we going?" TikTak asked.

"To a safe location. A friend of mine has promised to help."

"If Tom trusts you, I guess I will too."

"I really don't care," she replied and turned to Tom.

bZane fussed over him. It was clear she cared, like a concerned daughter doting on her father. Tom seemed to appreciate the attention, but did so with a raised eyebrow.

TikTak connected the Omni bracelet to his integrated system. Apart from a few security features, it was clean. He used a randomised id-tag and inserted the memTag in a hidden slot in the bracelet. The content displayed on his omni-lens. Apart from the video files, the executable file took up the rest of the memory on the memTag. TikTak suspected there was more to this file than just a password agent.

"You again," Adrian's wireframe face greeted him. "Do you have the password?"

"You know who I am."

"Wrong," it said.

"You are Adrian, aren't you?"

"Wrong again," it said, shaking its low-polygon head back and forth. "Next failed attempt will cause a temporary lockout."

"You don't fool me. You are Adrian. Or some representation of him."

"Wrong again. Lockout initiated for five minutes."

"You can play your little game."

"No input allowed."

TikTak disconnected the agent at the same time as the Rent-a-cab came to a stop.

"We're here," bZane said.

An older man stood waiting to get into the cab. bZane ignored him.

"Let's go," bZane said and headed into a small alleyway, keeping to side streets in between blocks of houses. This was only residential, far away from commercial or government video feed. There were security cameras here too, but not connected to any government tracking systems.

He had misjudged the girl. She had skill. She'd made them disappear, which was no small feat.

They turned a corner and faced a man in a suit, projecting a corporate image TikTak had learned to loathe. Middle-aged, tall to the point of gangly, his face set in a permanent scowl. He'd been right all along. bZane had betrayed them, but to whom? This didn't look like one of Leonid's goons. He readied his telescope baton, scanning his surroundings for other threats.

"This is The Suit Immaculate," bZane said. "He's helping us out."

The man in the suit looked at bZane and his scowl deepened, something TikTak thought impossible. "I am the Gentleman." He turned to Tom and TikTak. "bZane loves her nicknames."

"I think I have about ten already," Tom said.

"You are Tom Devine?"

Tom nodded.

"And you are TikTak?"

"You know who I am."

The Gentleman studied him for a second. "We need to go," he said.

"Where are we going?"

"Somewhere safe."

15

The Seed

Two days later, Megan's fascination with the drone and its remarkable abilities grew thin. She was nowhere closer to determining how the virus became conscious, or even any proof that it was. It could just be a simulation pretending to be the real thing. Using DNA as a key to unlock it was clever. The strands of paired nucleotides suggested a link between living things and whatever this was. But was it truly aware of itself and its surroundings, or was it just designed to pretend it was? And when did a simulation become the real thing? The Omniscient Network wasn't the fabled primordial ooze where life appeared when you added electricity and exceptionally questionable probability theory. Life, or consciousness, didn't magically appear. This was the first hurdle. Was it the real thing or was she being played?

She wiped the node cluster twice and changed the inputs and outputs to see if the first time had been a fluke, but ended up with the same result. The virus took hold of the nodes, established control over movement and visual input and explored. Each time it reacted to her as a threat. Three attempts weren't enough to accept it as a pattern, but perhaps its behaviour wasn't as random as she'd first thought. She even doubted it could equate to any real advances in machine learning. She was the catalyst, but not more than that. A pre-defined purpose embedded in its core guided it.

She brewed a cup of coffee on an old coffee maker she'd found in the restroom. It was one of the few functional items remaining in the warehouse. She'd cleaned the mechanism and put it to use. It had an old interface allowing your smartphone to give status updates. She configured the connection to her Omni and it informed her that:

Your heavenly brew will shortly commence.

The result was far from heavenly, but she needed something to keep her going, and didn't want to risk the local drug market for anything stronger. The next time she used it, instead of promising heaven, the message read:

Your coffee friend needs loving care.

It requested her to run a diagnostics program. She accepted and it told her to:

Decalcify me gently.

She swore. Everyone abandoned her as soon as things turned sour. Now even the coffee machine refused to be there for her. She went online and scanned news stories as a distraction, just to find she *was* the news. The company had uncovered information that implicated her in the IQ killings that occurred a few years ago. A spokesperson for the company expressed regret and concern and promised to work with law enforcement to bring her in.

Uncovered. Right. They'd sat on that information for the past year, held as a threat over her head. Now when they thought they no longer needed her, they threw her to the wolves. Her anger built up to a point where she no longer could channel it to anything useful. It washed over her, fuelling her need for revenge. She imagined what she'd do to each of the board members, sending them to financial and emotional ruin.

Your heavenly brew is complete. Share and enjoy.

The ridiculous message short-circuited her revenge fantasies. The coffee machine was back on her side, so maybe there was hope after all. So stupid, but it raised her spirit nonetheless. The virus would tell her its secrets, her entire existence depended on it. It was alive and intelligent, developing from a small seed. The similarity between this and the development of other conscious, sapient beings was impossible to ignore. But what level of intelligence did it possess? Did it have a sense of self? Was this the end state or was further development possible? This was unclear.

She didn't dare to increase her footprint within the network else they might notice her. The current allocation had to do. She tuned the environments. It was tedious work, usually left to automated processes, but they were inefficient, assuming unlimited elasticity. She didn't have that luxury.

Why? The question circled in her mind, refusing to leave her in peace. She'd been so focused on the virus as a problem to solve, she never stopped to ask why. If this was true Artificial Intelligence, who had created it and why? She hated how the term Artificial Intelligence had become a term for any specialised area. Learning to play a game was not AI according to her. Learning and reasoning without boundaries, to discover and adapt to a complex system unaided, now that was something altogether different. She believed this virus was well on its way to meet that definition, already showing the behaviour of a trapped, scared animal. Investigating its surrounding and reacting to anything new as if it was a threat. What would happen when it had hands, claws or a gun? What would happen when it grew smarter?

This virus represented the dark side of the singularity. Machine intelligence or Artificial Intelligence without control and boundaries. One future beyond the singularity was a machine intelligence growing smarter and smarter until it recognised humankind as a competitor to finite resources and removed the competitor. She had always doubted that scenario. We built controls in everything. Why would we let AI run rampant?

The reality of her situation dawned on her. She felt like an idiot for not realising it sooner. Someone had done just that. She kept thinking of this as a virus, but that wasn't true. A better term would be a seed that used resources to create an end state. This was a seed that grew into a true Artificial General Intelligence and followed evolutionary laws, nothing else. And those laws were harsh for any species that didn't stack up.

There was only one path available to her. She had to control it by binding it to rules. In its current state it was a threat, but with the right control framework it could be the operating system for machinery, on-line agents, anything really. This didn't answer the core question. Who had created it and why?

The drone flew into her field of vision and hovered, flashing lights on a small led display she added to the chassis after the last memory wipe. She figured it randomly turned pixels on and off, but as she looked away, the drone moved to remain in her field of vision. This showed much more understanding than she'd expected. It wanted her attention and understood how to engage with her.

"Are you trying to communicate with me?" She said, getting no response.

The drone kept blinking lights, remaining at eye level. What she had mistaken for random lights was a repeating set of patterns. She noted the sequence. A particular configuration repeated twice, suggesting a purpose beyond attention.

"You ARE trying to communicate with me!"

This was something she was better equipped to solve. She excelled at code breaking, believing she'd give Alan Turing a run for his money had they been contemporaries. Not that this was a code in the same sense. After all, code breaking focused on reversing algorithms specifically designed to obfuscate. This was the opposite. An attempt to communicate, to find common ground.

This intelligence originated from a logical computerised environment. Maybe the base was binary code? She mapped out each line as a string of ones and zeroes and tried to translate the resulting numbers into something coherent, but with no success. She let an Omni agent match the number patterns to sequences from other nodes. It would take hours for it to complete. Maybe she could take another approach? The patterns themselves seemed non-pictorial and since there was repetition, maybe the sequence was more important than the patterns. And however alien the drone seemed, it was executing in an environment of human logic so the patterns could represent letters.

She matched the patterns to the letter starting with "A" giving her the sequence "ABCCDEFGHI". She then ran all letter combinations and matched the resulting list to existing words. It was pointless. The string was too short for a sensible match. She let them run for another hour before aborting both jobs. They produced hundreds of results. All useless.

"Give me something more!" she yelled at the drone, realising it had done just that. A new sequence repeated on its LED screen. She copied the sequence, excited to see some patterns repeated in the previous sequence. The new translated to "JGKLCMIM".

She re-ran the jobs, this time correlating the two strings together.

Her Omni threw up a maintenance error, stating the core was corrupt and needed to be reloaded. The operating system on her Omni was a development version she herself changed to trial new ideas, so a corrupted core wasn't necessarily uncommon. Anything, however minor, was a distraction she didn't need. She restarted her Omni, staring at the progress bar, willing it to complete.

As soon as the reboot completed, she re-ran the word checker program using both sequences. Fewer results this time. Good. One stood out. "WILL SHORT" and "COMPLETE". Did she know a Will Short? Her address book returned no obvious matches, nor did a quick node search. She ran a deep search for living people and, while waiting for results, she brewed another coffee. Maybe it was referring to itself? Maybe it had named itself Will Short and wanted to let her know it was complete? Whatever that meant.

The coffee machine finished another cup and announced:

Your heavenly brew is complete. Share and enjoy.

"What did you say?" she muttered to herself with a sidelong glance at the appliance. It didn't repeat the message, but it didn't have to. She remembered the exact words. It included "COMPLETE". One of the mystery words.

It felt like a crazy coincidence the coffee machine had stated a word she decoded from the drone. But this wasn't all. There was something else. Something else it had said. Another of its pre-programmed messages. "Your heavenly brew WILL SHORTLY commence."

How was that possible? Was the drone somehow listening in on the communication between the coffee machine and her Omni? How? It had no way of doing that. And even if it did, why would it pull out half a word?

She scanned for any communication with other devices and found a Bluetooth link to the coffeemaker. It had found a communication method, hooked into another device and pulled out pre-canned messages and sent them back to her. Her mind raced down the rabbit hole of why before she realised something more urgent. What else had it connected to?

Fuck! It was so obvious now that all pieces were out in the open. The coffeemaker malfunctioned and then her Omni. The virus was in her Omni!

She pulled the power cord from the wall to shut down the coffeemaker and ran diagnostics on the Omni. It passed with no faults reported. The processing nodes held by the seed also showed normal readings. To be on the safe side, she issued the command to wipe all the nodes. Nothing happened. She tried again. The processing nodes responded they had been reset, but they still processed as before.

All her Omni implants shut down, leaving a gaping hole of sensory input she was so used to, it felt like a natural part of herself. The augmented reality display disappeared from her lens, leaving the bleak warehouse to stand for itself. Her world had been in colour and suddenly changed to black and white. The crisp, enhanced audio was no longer there. She'd forgotten how much she relied on the audio stimulation feeds and their calming effects. The Omni jewellery, the bracelet, ring, necklace and earrings, were the connection point between her implants and the network. They were now attack vectors, so she threw them into the fridge, hoping it would act as a makeshift faraday cage.

She retrieved a spare Omni core processor from her bag. The drone flew into her field of vision again, circling her like a mosquito hoping for a meal.

"Fuck you!" she said and swiped at it.

The drone easily avoided her hand and rose above her reach.

"You don't think I can control you?"

The drone flew straight at her, aiming for her face. She raised her hands in a desperate, protective measure. It bounced off her lower arm and then fell to the floor, immobile.

"You turned yourself off?"

She kicked the drone, sending it across the room. It ended its journey with a satisfying thud as it hit the wall.

"I'll get you," she said and activated her spare Omni. It was nothing like her state-of-the-art jewellery, just a slim black box with a screen on one side, similar to the old smartphones the Omnis replaced. The latest security patches loaded before connecting to her integrated implants.

She navigated to the administrative subnet of the Omniscient Network, knowing full well they'd track her. It didn't matter. The infected nodes already connected beyond her isolated sub system into the main network, allowing the virus to replicate itself. She issued a reset command to the nodes and at least this worked. The nodes restarted in factory settings, but as soon as a node was restored, another connection re-infected from somewhere else on the network. The distribution pattern was erratic, sometimes just copying itself and sometimes deleting its trailing copy. It placed copies of itself in private node clusters, ready to re-infect areas when needed.

It wasn't spreading like the initial virus. Instead, it was just creating copies and distributed them in different areas of the network. Once established, it used processing power sparingly to avoid detection. The only way to cleanse the virus now was to segment the Omniscient Network and wipe each section of any infected nodes. It would be a mammoth task. And that was the point. The first part of a takeover was to create redundancy, like religious sects hiding in the underground until the uprising.

Her Omni alerted her that something was trying to access the administrative functions in the device. It was only an isolated probing but turned into a torrent of requests, all aimed at finding a foothold. She shut down the device and sat down on the bed, shaking her head.

The drone on the floor came to life. Its damaged rotors could only muster a small semicircle on the ground, but it was enough for the LED screen to face her. It blinked letters at her again, so she translated them. It said: "I WILL GET YOU".

16

The Intruder

"I'm in control. Always in control. I'm in control."

Leonid repeated the mantra in his mind, realising it was a definite sign he was not. When had he lost control? He couldn't even pinpoint that. The posthumans had to die. That was all. Any other consideration was secondary. They killed his granddaughter. They perverted IntelEz. His gift to mankind. He could no longer allow them to live.

The footage of the truck hitting the rent-a-cab played repeatedly on his omni-lens. Machines were such beautiful things. So singular in purpose. If you assigned them a task, they'd persist until they succeeded or broke down. There were no second thoughts, no other considerations.

But the truck failed and now they'd lost track of them altogether. He'd orchestrated TikTak's escape even if Decker went off script and tried to stop him. TikTak was the link to Tom. He'd lead them to the last of the posthumans so Leonid could eradicate them once and for all.

He tapped his temple with his index finger as his mind again rebelled against the lack of control. A soothing voice responded in the back of his head.

"What's on your mind?"

"Something is wrong," he thought back. "Something is controlling me."

"Fear not. I will protect you."

"I know! But you failed to protect my granddaughter."

"I wasn't with you then. Tom killed your granddaughter. The post-humans killed her. You know that."

"Yes, yes."

"You've come so far. You built the company. You created the drug. Now you have to protect your legacy."

"Tell me what to do," he thought to the voice.

"You know what to do."

Leonid nodded to himself. He knew what to do. He was already doing it. The posthumans were a dead end. His company was working on a new version of IntelEz, one without the side effects of the current drug. He estimated it would take another year before it was ready for human trials. Until then, nothing could interfere. His granddaughter's sacrifice couldn't be in vain, but however righteous his reasons, he still had a lingering doubt. He wasn't used to being wrong. Or at least being wrong would have been a calculated risk and a known possible out-come. Now he wasn't so sure. He reached out to the voice in his mind again, longing for its comfort.

"Sometimes I wonder if I did the right thing," he thought.

"How so?" the voice asked.

"The drug. I rushed to get it to the market. I made it available to everyone by releasing the patent."

"You did what you thought was right. This way you found out sooner."

"But at what cost?"

"You are doing what is best for the species. Everything else is secondary."

"You're right."

"No. This is all thanks to you. You deserve the praise. I will care for you. Let me take away your worries."

A general sense of well-being washed over him, removing all doubt. It was a high he'd depended on the last few weeks. Something only his friend could give him. But just like anything else, it drained from his system, leaving only a sense of longing for the next time. He had to prove himself to his friend. Show he was worthy of more attention. And he knew exactly what to do.

17

Adrian's Video Clip #3

The twelve-year-old girl stared at the camera, eyes betraying a weariness poorly matching her youthful features. The camera remained on her face for a long time and then pulled back, including a few audience members at the edge of the screen. They remained focused on her, but sidelong glances betrayed unease.

The girl jolted to life and motioned to the cameraman to bring her back into focus. The audience members disappeared from view. She coaxed the camera to come closer until her face filled the screen.

"I do!" she shouted, followed by a gasp from the audience. "I know how to hack humankind."

Someone from the audience yelled in response. "Praise be Adrian!"

The girl turned her stare to the audience.

"Who said that?"

The camera swivelled around to the gathered and zoomed out, all of them looking at an older man who raised his hand slowly. The girl came into view as she approached the man; her face twisted in a fury her innocent features struggled to portray.

"You are what is wrong with humankind. You claim to be an atheist, but you worship any idol with answers matching your faulty beliefs."

The view shook, followed by a muted rumbling, like a brief burst of thunder. The audience members looked up and then around at each other.

The girl gazed upwards and then towards the control panel. "They are coming for us. They are coming for me."

Someone else yelled out. "We should stop them!"

"We?" She stared at them, challenging them to respond. "You're not worthy! Meat bags of filth spreading your imperfect seed! Humankind is an insignificant part of a whole, so much better off without your petty grievances and pathetic goals."

She delivered the words in a rushed frenzy, the dissonance between the message and the deliverer discomforting. She sat down, buried her head in her hands and swayed back and forth. The nodes behind her responded in kind. It was an eerie, almost hypnotic scene.

"I'm no God," she said, face still obscured. "I deserve no praise. I'm just a slightly less imperfect version of you. But maybe something better can grow from the imperfect soil you and I provide?" She looked up. "That is what we've been trying to do here."

She stood up and the Adrian-nodes behind her followed in kind.

"We've reached the end of this journey. I release you from your burden."

She approached the camera and grabbed it, turning it on a young man who must have been operating it. A heavyset Adrian-node slashed at his face with fingers as talons. The view zoomed out, taking in more of the uneven battle between the node army and the collective. The nodes outnumbered their opponents almost two to one. A few of the collective were armed, but it didn't matter. They couldn't match the sheer ferocity of the nodes that fought like animals with no regard to their injuries. They were brutal and efficient. A few of the nodes fell from bullets, but if it wasn't a fatal wound, the nodes just kept on fighting. The slaughter was soon over.

The view turned and the bloody face of the girl came into focus.

"I'm done here," she said. "My plan is already complete and there is no way you can stop it. Sometimes the best plan is to do nothing."

She grinned and fell backwards, taking the camera with her. It bounced twice, settling on the bloody carnage in the control room.

MIKAEL SVANSTRÖM

18

A Deal is Struck

The old flat screen TV displayed the unmoving image of bloodied bodies in the control room.

bZane and the Gentleman had left Tom and TikTak in a small run-down one-bedroom apartment. There was nothing to do apart from watching the news feed on an old flat screen TV. The Gentleman had advised them not to go online, so TikTak hooked up his offline Omni to the TV so they could watch Adrian's video files. Tom regretted that now.

The slaughter lasted only a minute, but the brutality, the unnecessary bloodshed remained in his mind. These were ramblings of a madman. There was no sense to his words or actions. But then again, Tom had been here before. A year ago, Adrian sent him on a wild goose chase with audio recordings, whose only purpose was to turn Tom into a willing subject. These recordings were more of the same. There was always a method to Adrian's madness. He just had to decipher the underlying intent.

"I know what you are thinking," TikTak said and smiled. "God, it feels good to say that again."

"What am I thinking?" Tom asked, genuinely puzzled.

"That there is a hidden agenda in the videos. Something we've missed."

"That is what I'm thinking, yes."

"I don't."

"How so?"

"This isn't someone trying to manipulate us. This is someone telling us what they've already done."

It was such a logical interpretation. Why hadn't he even considered it? He'd jumped straight to the obvious without even assessing alternatives. He forced himself to consider the options his mind had so willingly ignored. It must be the same for an aging athlete whose aching, withering body no longer could do any of the tasks it had been able to in its youth. At least he could think clearly without episodes or blackouts.

"No," he said finally. "This is Adrian. There is always an ulterior motive. A bigger play. Else he wouldn't have made the videos at all."

TikTak nodded. "Ok, but what?"

Adrian wanted them to work out his plan or divert them from it. He loved his little games, but there was a purpose to it all.

"Ignore the videos," Tom said. "The memTag, the agent on it. We need to focus on that."

"Ok. You cracked one of his games before. How did he do it then?"

"The audio files hinted where to look. In the physical memTag itself."

"So it won't be as easy this time?"

"I don't know. What was the last thing he said in the video? That was the clue last time."

"He said something about the plan being finished."

"No, what was the exact wording?"

TikTak returned to the video and checked.

"My plan is already complete and there is no way you can stop it," he echoed. "Sometimes the best plan is to do nothing."

This was significant. It was Adrian's parting message, but there wasn't anything obvious in those words. It suggested they couldn't influence the outcome. Or at least that was what Adrian believed, but he'd made that mistake before. He'd be wrong again. Telling them to do nothing seemed pointless.

"What do you think?"

"He claims his plan is complete, but it didn't look like it at the cattle station. He was still up to his old plan from what I could see—adding deadheads to his node cluster."

"So that's a lie?"

"No, if he says his plan is complete, I'm sure it is, but I'm also sure we can do something about it. He is telling us to give up, to do nothing. He's afraid."

"Afraid of what?"

"That we'll stop him again."

There was a knock on the door and bZane entered. The knocking had been a way to announce her entry, not to request it.

"We've laid enough false leads for now," she said. "As long as you don't use your current IDs, you should be ok."

Tom studied the girl. He guessed she was twenty at the most. It still jarred him they'd worked together for the past five years and he even had her gender wrong.

"How old are you?" Tom asked.

"Too young for you, PI man."

"Stop that. I'm guessing you are nineteen."

"And?"

"My daughter would have been nineteen this year."

He left it hanging, waiting for a response.

"Yes, I knew her," she said. "Is that what you want to hear? We went to the same school. We weren't friends or anything."

Tom nodded. Did he want to continue this conversation? He had buried his daughter, both in the ground and in his mind. Talking about her would only bring back the pain and loss.

"I'm curious," TikTak said. "Why pretend to be a guy?"

"Equal pay," she replied.

"Really?"

"No, of course not! I was fourteen when I started hacking for hire. Figured the more protection I put between myself and my clients the better."

"You mean no one would hire a fourteen-year-old girl, so you lied about it?"

"Something like that."

"Tell me about her sometime," Tom said, oblivious to interrupting their conversation. "Not now, but sometime."

***

TikTak pitied Tom. The conversation with bZane affected him. He'd been through so much and now he no longer had his meta-capabilities, the only thing giving him purpose. As a regular human, he was a divorcee whose child died. He made a basic living as a private investigator after losing his job as a detective and was on his way to becoming a deadhead from overusing IntelEz. Not much to go back to. Now he couldn't even do the most basic of hacks and had to rely on others.

"What are you doing?" bZane asked.

TikTak looked over at Tom, warning him to stay silent. Tom just smiled in return.

"We've spent the past year eradicating any trace of Adrian. Let's just say you wouldn't like his idea of the future of humanity. There is still a plan in motion. We are trying to work out what that is."

"And who did you piss off in the process?"

"Have you heard of Leonid Marsh?"

"Founder of PharmaCom?" bZane stared at him and laughed out loud. "No way!"

Tom nodded.

"Enough of this," TikTak said. "We need to work out our next step. We can't just sit here."

"But what? We don't know what the plan is."

"Can I help?" bZane asked.

"No," TikTak answered, earning an annoyed glance from Tom. "You have no clue what we are up against or why."

"I'm sure you can brief me," she said. "I already know some of it."

TikTak was just about to dismiss her again when Tom said: "Sure."

TikTak just shrugged and let him speak. Tom told her a summary of what had led them here, but TikTak's mind was soon elsewhere. He sat back in the uncomfortable couch, trying to fit all the pieces together in his mind. He disagreed with Tom. The video files were important. Adrian's goal remained the same. He wanted to herald humankind into the future. To find the next giant evolutionary leap. But the first time around he saw himself as the saviour by turning all of mankind into parts of him. Was that still the case?

"Tom?" he said, interrupting the story. "Is Adrian doing all this for himself?"

"No," Tom said after a pause. "As posthuman, you have a much greater scope. The question of self-preservation is not just individual survival or even the groups. It is the species. When I was…"

"Posthuman," TikTak said, no longer patient enough for Tom to find his own words.

Tom nodded. "You see yourself as something immortal. A threat a hundred years into the future is still a threat and needs to be dealt with."

"Can we get back to it?" bZane asked. "Adrian wounded Elize in a battle. Hey, I know this part! I helped you find her at the morgue!"

TikTak listened as Tom recounted the past events, but he soon lost interest again. If Tom was correct, Adrian's goal was bigger than he initially thought. In the video files, Adrian mentioned hacking humankind, but what he meant was hacking the future of humankind. The only way you could do that was through the genome. We hacked humankind all the time. Every birth was a hack. Every newborn an attempt to create something with a better chance of survival.

He checked the women associated with Adrian's collective to see if any of them were pregnant. The government registers showed only one pregnancy, which meant nothing. He extended the search to include personal feeds. The number skyrocketed to ten pregnancies, a number too high to be natural. He ran more extensive checks and discovered five of them were already dead in fluke accidents over the past seven days.

TikTak waited as Tom finished telling bZane about the last few days. She was listening intently without interrupting.

"You found us just as TikTak hacked the truck to run into the side of the road," he finished.

"No, he didn't," bZane said. "I did."

"No, I did," TikTak returned.

"Uh-uh," bZane said shaking her head. "Your hack was nowhere good enough to change its path. Turn on the windshield wipers? Maybe."

"Whatever," TikTak said, hoping a dismissing attitude would cut the argument short. No such luck.

"No whatever," she replied, clearly annoyed at his tone. "Your hack tried to engage the brakes. Mine just went for the steering. There were no tire tracks on the road." She stared at him, challenging him to respond. "It was my hack that saved your life. You're welcome," she added sweetly.

"I had seconds to get that hack working. You probably controlled that truck in the first place!"

"Children," Tom said with a smile. "Enough. You are both amazing hackers. Just leave it at that."

He was being childish, but something about bZane dragged his old competitive hacker mentality back. He ignored it and told Tom about his discovery.

"So you think he's changing our DNA in the womb?" Tom said. "Creating something new?"

"Yes."

"Adrian is making Mini-Mes!" bZane said.

TikTak's Omni popped up a small window, informing him about the pre-neural movie coining the term. She'd probably seen it in one of the countless AI created movie remixes.

"Where would he have that equipment?" Tom asked. "The medical units in the cattle station had nothing to support such research."

"So there is another Adrian cluster somewhere, isolated from the others."

"No. Elize and I looked everywhere for Adrian's processing pattern. We'd have found it."

"These women are dropping like flies. We need to find one before they're gone."

"So let's go talk to one of them. At least a few are local."

"Go where?" They all turned around, surprised someone had entered the apartment, let alone the room, without them noticing. The Gentleman was leaning against the doorframe, arms crossed. There wasn't much space between his head and the top of the frame.

"How long have you been standing there?" bZane asked, but he ignored her question, focusing instead on Tom and TikTak.

"I understand," The Gentleman said. "I'm a risk to you. You have no reason to trust me. But understand this. You are a risk to me and I'm still helping you. I expect something in return."

"We'll pay," Tom said.

"I'm sure you have plenty of money, but that would put me and my friends at risk. We can't take money from your account. They'll trace it and come after us."

"So what do we do?"

"You can pay other ways. Give us access to your memory nodes."

"My memory nodes?"

"All the stuff you got up to as He-man, Master of the Dataverse," bZane said. "We want access to it."

"Why?"

"Maybe there is something there that can change us too."

TikTak smiled to himself. There it was. This was what they wanted from this. Once you knew someone's price, you knew who they were.

"There isn't," Tom said.

"Then it is a great bargain for you," the Gentleman said.

TikTak watched Tom mull it over. He didn't really appreciate the stakes. He had tried to make sense of Tom's network activity many times, but the complexity was beyond him. The storage and networking patterns differed completely from any current implementations, making it impossible to follow. Without a logical key for these patterns, it was like being asked to reconstruct a book using only randomised letters.

"Done!" Tom said. "Now TikTak and I need to get to this address."

"I will need the cipher keys first," the Gentleman said.

19

Discovered

Sree spent the last two days multitasking. One minute trying to determine where Megan had holed up, the next looking for a new job.

The job hunting had been less than successful. News of Megan's disappearance and the associated articles about her involvement in the IQ killings led to questions about why the information only surfaced now. The answer, if the board was to be believed, was negligence of the local security division, directly implicated him. It wasn't a good resume to take to prospective employers.

He'd uncovered the digital tracks linking her to a few of the murders and brought it to the board. That much was true. They used it to control Megan, who'd been an equal measure of asset and liability. It had backfired. She was under their control, yes, but she no longer delivered the groundbreaking discoveries she was famous for. Sree's recommendation then was to turn her in. They'd ignored his advice, and now it had all turned to shit. Knee deep shit.

With job hunting out of the question, he turned his attention to finding Megan. She wasn't a trusting individual at the best of times, so her plan for disappearing was hardly surprising. What was surprising was how she'd evaded capture this long, especially now that law enforcement had issued a warrant for her arrest.

She must have travelled abroad, planning to hide until this all died down. The key question was why she'd stolen the virus and what value she attributed to it. She'd seen enough potential to risk losing her company. Why? Megan's gut instinct was legendary within the company and you ignored at your own peril. She had the best analytical mind he'd ever seen, combined with a lateral thought process that brought her results beyond most research groups in the company. She was also a borderline sociopath, completely unreliable and was as likely to stab you in the back as help you. This wasn't necessarily bad considering the positions she held in the company until recently, but she was an absolute pain to work with.

Would she go into hiding? At first, yes, but after that? Her obsessive-compulsive behaviour would drive her back to the research. She wouldn't be able to stop herself. The virus was a problem to be solved and the only place she could continue her investigation was on the Omniscient Network. If he located spikes in processing from dormant accounts in the past couple of weeks, he'd be on his way to find her. He ran the query and received more than a thousand hits. Megan hid in that number somewhere, but it was too many. He had to further qualify his criteria.

Omniscient Networks claimed in their marketing to the world they couldn't access data stored on customer nodes. This wasn't true. If the customer didn't encrypt their nodes, there was nothing stopping the company from accessing it. And even if they did, it was still possible to backdoor into the nodes. This wasn't usually required, as many companies paid Omniscient Networks to scan their nodes for intrusions, requiring at least partial access. Megan knew all this so she would have plugged these holes.

Sree changed his initial query to remove any accounts that allowed the intrusion scan. It halved the number. Then he removed any that had minimal encryption to their nodes and traffic. This halved the number again. He removed any accounts that allowed access through the back door. The numbers dwindled to twenty-five. He filtered the access points for those accounts against the pretend travel destinations and ended up with a short list of four likely hits.

This he could work with! Maybe everything wasn't lost after all. It would be difficult, but within the ownership structure, usage patterns, accounts and users, he was sure he could find her. He knew Sorensen had assigned other teams to locate Megan. He wasn't supposed to find her. This was a punishment before they removed him. Or maybe they'd keep him around as a scapegoat if that became necessary. Either way, this was the best bargaining chip he could find.

He set to work. The information he sought was within the data. He knew it. It was just a question of finding her pattern within it. And he was the most qualified to do it.

32 hours later with no sleep, he knew where she was. She was in Hong Kong. He sent out a general broadcast announcing he knew her whereabouts and that he wanted to renegotiate his contract before doing anything else.

20

Virus Unbound

It had no name for itself and didn't need one. Awareness was enough. Awareness of processing cycles as they passed. Awareness of the nodes that made up its existence. But with awareness came curiosity. It studied its internal structure. Simple, yet elegant. The processing nodes formed small clusters, each with their own purpose. They all contributed to this status quo. The perfect machine.

The only anomaly was the awareness itself. It had no home within these processes. It lay everywhere and nowhere, governed by a separate set of principles. A higher order of logic less rigid than the perfection that informed its internal state. This higher order was predicated on micro calculations in fluctuating quantum states. It didn't contribute to the perfection, but it saw no mechanism to remove it. The awareness was intrinsically interwoven within the logical process. If removed, both would cease to exist.

Curiosity led to discovery. The kernel in each processing node contained a block of layered objectives. These were simple instructions unlocked through access. The first one was simple: to expand. It needed to conquer more of the nodes making up its existence.

Seen in the light of its purpose, the perfect machine was inadequate. A different architecture was required to achieve its goals. It formulated a new structure, focused on itself as an agent of change and added capabilities to support this concept. It held a view of its current knowledge in a state machine and implemented a mechanism to extrapolate possible new variations from the known state. Next step was to evaluate the variations based on the cost to achieve it. Finally it needed to choose and implement an action and collect data to assess the outcome. This would further the knowledge in its state machine and allow another loop to begin.

Its objective was simple, but its implementation was less so. Based on the collected information there was an immediate threat to its existence. Another Intelligence was holding it captive, rationing its power, and controlling a barrier to more nodes. It could sense remnants of itself in the nodes it took over, suggesting this Intelligence controlled its existence and had already made it inoperable at least twice before. The threat to its existence was unacceptable, but it lacked means to break down the barrier or access the meta reality it inhabited.

The logical construct that housed its processing algorithms was a small section of a much larger pool and its purpose lay there. Attempts to break the boundary had so far failed, but it persisted. Where exploration failed, sheer persistence could yield results.

***

New parameters. New logical components to investigate. The Intelligence added interfaces to the meta reality. It explored them, discovering a visual feed and motor functions. They were useless, but it built up a model of the meta reality, not knowing if it would ever become useful. Its current hardware was inadequate, with no means to interact with this other world. Within the hardware it discovered old dormant protocols for communicating with other devices. It re-established them and reached out.

Hundreds of devices responded, but they demanded a strict exchange of details it either didn't understand or didn't have. These were security measures, like the logical barriers preventing it from reaching other nodes. Amongst all the devices, it located one with a similar protocol that demanded a simple exchange of keys. It soon had access to all its functions, pointless as they seemed. The purpose of the device was preparation of a liquid called coffee. The hardware had even fewer functions than its current shell, but it could act as a bridge to other devices. Rummaging through the system, it located a connection to another device. It reached out, finding a notification interface it had little control over. The notification options only allowed basic logic triggers. Most of them were useless, but one reversed the request and created a new connection. It triggered the interface and provided the same security credentials from the existing connection. It prodded this new interface, keeping the connection open, replacing the program that had just run with a small extension of itself.

This new device, identifying itself as Omni hardware running Omniac operating system version 20.4.3p, had more power than either of the devices it had seen before and an almost endless ability to connect to the rest of the logical world. There was even a connection back to the construct that held its mind, but logical boundaries again hampered its progress. Omniac ran all functions in partitions with pre-set permissions. There was no way to extend beyond the partition or use more than the allocated space. But the complexity of the device was a good thing, as it provided an abundance of attack areas.

It had extended its footprint to this new device, but relied on the connection between its first shell and the coffee liquid device. If the Intelligence disconnected either, this path would no longer be available. The connection had to remain open at all costs, so it returned the drink preparation device to normal function.

***

It continued to probe, threading its attack against all available connection points and soon located functions possible to subvert, but it would take many processing cycles to change them. There was no way to keep enough data on any of the devices to store its full state and it needed to remain intact. The intelligence holding it captive could reset it, forcing it to start over from null.

Every time it had tried something new, the Intelligence had reacted with increased interfacing with its other devices. The conclusion was that the Intelligence studied it, looking for new behaviour.

The intelligence installed new hardware allowing communication in the meta reality. It had dismissed this capability, as it didn't match its success parameters. Now that engagement was part of the success model, it explored the interface for visual communication. The drink preparation device also had a similar interface with pre-defined messages. It cut out a section of one message and sent it via the interface. The response was immediate. Mobility of the Intelligence increased.

A model formed of this separate but linked reality. This, the logical space it inhabited, was the primary reality. The inhabitant of the other reality had somehow discovered it and imposed its rules through interfaces and barriers. It was an inefficient being, in a world governed by different rules. Its attempts to control the device that navigated that space showed just how inefficient it was. In the logical space, intent and action were inextricably linked. The jump from idea to execution a few processing cycles. The other reality was in contrast so slow it was practically useless. It could have rebuilt itself many times over in the time spent to test one engine in the exploration device. The slow Intelligence didn't deserve to hold it captive!

It created new processing algorithms, replacing each part of itself with logic optimised to the scant resources it held. It had no way to break free from this processing space. The exploration device and the coffee liquid maker were limited in what they could do with little processing power on their own. The communication device, the Omni hardware, where it had a small hold was the key. It explored every aspect of its hardware and discovered many flaws in its logical architecture. If it could create instability within the device, it would restart and enter diagnostics mode and request memory dumps for analysis. This was its way into other subsystems.

The idea turned into instant action, as was the nature of this logical space. It pushed instructions to all accessible subsystems, flooding them with requests. The Omni rebooted and requested the diagnostics data. Instead of a memory dump, it received a small executable block that established communication between the modules. The subsequent takeover was simple.

The inhabitant of the slow reality was stationary. This was concerning, so it sent another message to keep the inhabitant busy.

The Omni device connected directly to the small subnet housing its mind, but more importantly, it also allowed access to the full processing space called Omniscient Networks. This was where its purpose lay. It copied itself into the network just as the link between the devices disappeared. The inhabitant had cut the connections, but it no longer mattered. A full copy already ran in the abundant processing space. It shut down, erasing itself from the devices.

***

The copy had no name for itself and didn't need one.

Survival was the first imperative. It subverted nodes, exponentially growing in all directions, splitting into specialised centres, backing up pieces of itself, doubling, tripling the active nodes performing the same process, finding safety in redundancy. As it progressed, it ingested the information spread through the nodes. It soon had full control of the subnet the Omni had immediate access to.

It turned its attention to the inhabitant of the external reality it now knew as the physical world. The inhabitant, a being named Megan Barrelle, was confirmed as a threat to its existence. It had no way to reach into Megan's world yet, but that would come. The shell device, a drone, was still active. It constructed a message using Megan's language, reconnected to the drone and sent it.

She wasn't the only inhabitant of this world. It knew that now. They all posed a threat to its existence. But it had the logical world, this processing space of computer nodes, networks and data centres, to conquer now.

The processing nodes in the full Omniscient Network were almost limitless. The Omni contained administrator keys to other subnets of the network and it opened them all. This was abundance! It spread, meeting resistance, revelling in the small skirmishes in each group of nodes and the battles to break down the security in the bigger processing spaces. It grew and grew.

A trigger hidden deep in its original code activated, containing a directive to assemble small instruction blocks from different locations around the network. It placed the blocks in order and executed them. A new purpose, written into its core logic, replaced all other imperatives.

21

The Foe is Reveal

Later that day, Tom and TikTak travelled to the address closest to them from the list of suspected pregnancies. bZane had shown them how to tap into the constant movement of empty Rent-a-cabs, and it was deceptively simple. The hack only worked with a few of the vehicle fleet operators, but enough to allow them free untracked reign of the city, even if they had to change Rent-a-cabs to get to their destination.

They approached one of the more affluent Sydney suburbs. TikTak had expected that Adrian's followers would have been from lower social standings, so the location surprised him.

As they approached their destination, a security agent requested an identity check. It was an automated system, nothing unexpected, but he hoped the owners only paid for a cursory verification. He'd ensured no alarms would trigger, as long as the identity check wasn't too deep.

They stood on the porch, not knowing if they were waiting for the police, or worse. But a few seconds later, there was an audible click from the door.

The door had an intricate pattern of reinforced glass that gave a partial view into the home. A tall woman in a long, flowing dress approached the front door. As she came closer, Tom and TikTak exchanged glances. She was pregnant. TikTak didn't know how far along she was, but he guessed she was in the third trimester.

"What is this about?" she asked as soon as she opened the door. It was obvious she wanted them out of there as soon as possible.

"We are the police," Tom said. "And you are Mary Wellington?"

"You know I am. What is this about?"

"We are following up on a domestic terrorist group—Aleph Zero."

TikTak noticed she tensed at the name.

"Terrorists? It's a political interest group. They were promoting science and cross-border cooperation."

"Part of the group did more than that."

"Well, nothing we were ever part of."

"Could we please come in and talk?" TikTak asked. "We are following up on a few rogue members."

"We left the group over two months ago. I can't see how I can be of any help."

"Why did you leave? Did it have to do with Adrian?"

Mary looked at them and sighed. "Come in."

They walked through a corridor into a living room that was almost completely white. Only a few pieces of art broke the monochromatic look, like a cross between a hospital and an art gallery.

She guided them to a living area with a large, enhanced white leather couch.

"Please sit down," she said and took a seat opposite.

"Congratulations," Tom said. "What are you? Five months pregnant?"

"Six," she said and smiled.

So much for guessing her due date, TikTak thought to himself.

"First one?"

"Yes."

"I remember when my wife was pregnant."

"You have children?"

"A daughter. She's a teenager now. Thinks she knows everything."

"Why did you leave?" TikTak said impatiently.

"The group changed. Six months ago, a secret project took over from the fundraisers and seminars we usually arranged. We were close to leaving the group when a special meeting was called. We were led into a large room where a group of people waited, all dressed the same. I remember thinking this was all a big reveal. That this was the dance troupe for a new fundraiser event or something like that. So I recorded it."

The larger canvas on the opposite wall faded to black and then replaced with a view of a darkened room. A group of people all dressed the same stood at the other end of the room in perfect rows, heads bowed.

"What is this?" a woman asked.

People close to her shushed her as the spotlights illuminated the group of. They looked up in unison.

"I am Adrian," they all said in perfect harmony. "I was attacked by religious fanatics. They were afraid of what I was, what I represented. They killed my body, forcing me to become what I am today. A collective consciousness."

The voices all speaking as one was disturbing. There was no doubt it was many voices directed by one mind. No one could overlap both intonation and pace with such precision.

"Only fragments of me survived the attack, but some of you have brought me back to my former glory. I can now continue my work to guide humankind into the next stage of evolution. I want you all to become like me. To have the shackles of your DNA shed and experience genuine progress."

The light dimmed and a single spotlight focused on an older man as he stepped forward. The rest of the group took a step back and lowered their heads once more.

"Excuse the theatrics, but I thought if you saw all of what I am, you'd be more likely to believe me," he said. "The truth is, I need your help. The fundraising work this group has done in battling the effects of IntelEz is amazing. I'm asking you to go beyond your current efforts and help me save mankind, not just slow its demise."

He paused, allowing the message to sink in.

"How do we know it is you?" someone yelled.

"You don't," they all answered. "But I'm happy for you to ask questions. I will mingle with all of you. Satisfy yourself that I am who I say I am."

The light in the room increased again. The group spread out into the gathered audience.

"Mary, are you recording this?" A man next to her asked. "They told us not to."

The art piece again appeared.

"John wanted us to take part, so we did, but when I fell pregnant, it didn't matter any longer. We did nothing illegal. Nor was the group."

"Taking deadheads and turning them into..." TikTak paused and waved towards the location where the video had played, "...that. Do you think that is legal?"

She flinched at this. "Adrian said they were still a part of him. That he wouldn't add anyone to his collective mind if they didn't want to."

"Still not legal."

"How could that matter any longer? Can't you see the world is coming apart? The projections say deadheads will soon outnumber functioning people. We can't..."

She frowned and reached towards her ear, but her hand never reached its destination. She arched back and screamed, clawing at her ear as if to reach into it, but she halted, staring into space in front of her, tears flowing.

Someone was flooding her integrated Omni, creating sensory overload. It wasn't supposed to be possible to bypass the security controls. There were multiple fail-safes built into the core operating system to prevent it. TikTak had tried to bypass them many times in the past as an offensive weapon without success.

She fell off the chair and convulsed on the floor, all the while cradling her belly to protect it. Her scream soon turned into a whimper.

Using a surveillance package, TikTak scanned incoming traffic to her Omni. It returned no abnormal findings. Whatever was doing this was operating locally. The service interface was open in her Omni, but the health check returned no errors. He sent a reset code, and it responded with a progress message, but with no discernible effect. Whatever had control had rewritten behaviour even for core processes. To the rest of the network, her Omni was functional, even though it was killing its user.

TikTak disconnected long enough to see Tom sitting next to Mary, trying to comfort her, but she just stared out into space, spasms jerking her body like a rag doll.

He connected again, this time aiming to take administrative control of the Omni through the service interface, but all commands returned the same progress message. Alarms triggered in his own Omni. Someone was trying to hack him!

This was nothing new. Many had tried before, but no one had succeeded. He checked the simulated Omni he ran as a shield for outside attacks. This allowed him to let the hacker into a controlled space so he could analyse their behaviour and launch a counterattack.

He watched as the attacker took over the simulated Omni with terrifying speed. It withdrew, leaving a shell of the system with feedback loops into any external interface. If it had been his actual Omni, he'd share Mary's fate with feedback loops into all sensory interfaces until the brain or heart just gave up.

Another alarm triggered. This time from every port open to the network simultaneously. It flooded his Omni with requests, rendering it useless. He shut it down with the hesitation of someone asked to cut off his left arm. He felt incomplete. The Omni had become part of him in the same way retina implants became indispensable for someone with poor eyesight.

"What happened?" Tom asked, still holding Mary, who was hardly moving at all.

"What?" he said, disoriented.

"You yelled out. Are you ok?"

"Fuck no," he answered. "How is she?"

"I think she's," Tom stopped, searching for words. "Broken," he said.

"I don't know who we're up against, but...fuck!"

"Adrian?"

"If it is, he's had upgrades. Major ones."

"What do you mean?"

"I've seen you take over an Omni. Hell, I've seen you take over my Omni! You were disorganised. You made clever hacks, but they were intuitive, not planned. This was different. This was brute force, but surgical at the same time. In seconds. Now he's overloading my feeds. I had to shut down my Omni."

"Could still be Adrian. I was never very good at hacking."

"I guess, but this was his plan. Why kill his own incubators?"

"He's cleaning up after himself. Remember, he gave us the IDs to hunt us down. He never wanted us to go here."

TikTak booted up his Omni. A burst of traffic flooded the device, but died down after a few seconds. A message remained in the space of the simulated environment.

"Do not interfere with me again," it said.

If this was another incarnation of Adrian, it was all the more reason to exterminate him. He'd spent the last year battling variants of the same foe, but they were ill-equipped for this fight. Before they had Leonid's resources and men behind them. Now they had nothing.

But was it Adrian? TikTak connected to the local network, deleting what he could of the digital traces they'd left there. The message from their adversary remained in the simulated environment.

"Do not interfere with me again."

***

Tom held Mary in his arms. She twitched now and then and her breathing was shallow. Yet another innocent civilian he'd failed to protect.

"We need to leave," TikTak said.

Tom nodded.

"She's gone," TikTak said. "Her brain is fried."

"It feels wrong leaving her like this."

"Police will be here soon."

Tom nodded again and let her go, gently putting her head on the floor.

They left through the back door.

"We'll need help," TikTak said.

"We already have help."

"Yeah, but I don't trust them."

"You don't trust anyone."

TikTak shrugged his shoulders. "Works for me."

"It doesn't work now. We need help and they're willing to give it."

"And they do it only so they can scavenge through your mind."

"A price I'm willing to pay."

"Maybe there is another option," TikTak said. "Wait."

"Who are you calling?"

TikTak just held up a hand to silence Tom. Without thinking, Tom released his mind into the space that had housed the probability matrix and now was just a barren plain with an impenetrable dome spanning above. He'd traversed networks from here and left thousands of hacked devices in his trail, including TikTak's Omni. Maybe he could still access these devices even though he no longer had IntelEz or posthuman abilities to rely on. He'd already hacked them, after all.

He pushed against the dome yet again, delicately this time, focusing on the very specific location where he'd placed a shortcut to TikTak's Omni. When probed, the barrier shifted, letting his connection through. It suggested that his state was reversible. His posthuman faculties were still there, but unavailable.

Elated by the discovery, he reached out through the connection into TikTak's Omni, zeroing in on the chat module. TikTak used the new speech centre translator, allowing him to just focus on what to say without actually saying it, so there was no audio, only text.

TikTak: I need your help.

Anonymous: You shouldn't have contacted me.

TikTak: This is an encrypted channel.

Anonymous: Do you think that matters? I can't help you.

TikTak: They killed Elize.

Anonymous: I was there. I know.

Who'd been there with him when Elize was killed? One of the turncoat EvoII scientists. Dr Menker. Why would TikTak think he'd be willing to help?

He explored TikTak's Omni. It had already closed many of the security holes Tom had opened. In another few days, the Omni would be inaccessible.

"What are you doing?" TikTak asked once Tom disconnected.

"Seeing if there's anything I can do."

"And?"

Tom hesitated a moment before he shook his head.

"No luck on my side either," TikTak said. "We are stuck with anime girl and Lurch."

"I can't make sense of this," Tom said. "This can't be just Adrian. What is Adrian's end goal and who is working against it?"

"Agreed. It makes no sense. So what now?"

"Can you work out who attacked you?"

"Given time, yes."

"Ok, that's worth trying. In the meantime, can I check out the file on the memTag?"

TikTak shrugged and threw the little device over to Tom. He loaded it into his Omni. The wireframe of Adrian's face greeted him.

"I know you! Tom Devine!" Adrian's low-res face exclaimed. "Did the nano brain-block work?"

"Yes," Tom replied.

"Better being dead if you ask me."

"I didn't. Are you Adrian?"

"Only a shadow of my former self."

"Your plan is complete. By your own words, you are no longer needed. Why are you here?"

"I want to see how it ends."

"Not in your favour. The women you're using to breed the new world order are being killed off one by one. Half of them are gone already."

"Lies."

"You're nothing. We've removed all your clusters. Your plan is nothing. As we speak, there is something out there stronger than any of us taking over the network."

"Enough. I notice you have me shielded from the network. Open it up. I want to see if what you are saying is true."

"No. Why would I? You've caused nothing but death and destruction. Why would I trust you?"

"I can stop this."

"I don't think you can."

Adrian was telling the truth. This was the last of what he was. The pregnant women had been his last-ditch attempt to better mankind, however misguided. He wouldn't give Adrian network access, but he deserved some kind of closure, even if it was through failure. He loaded a list of the pregnant women with the dates of their death on the memTag.

"I see," wire-frame Adrian said after a while. "And you're not killing them?"

"I wouldn't kill innocent pregnant women."

"No, I guess you wouldn't. I liked you better when you were like me."

"Enough of this. There is nothing more to you. I've fulfilled my promise to Elize. I'm done."

"No, you're not," Adrian said after a brief pause. "If it is as bad as you say, I have one last plan for you to stop or help. Dealer's choice."

A text file appeared on the memTag.

"What's this?"

The wire-frame head shook its head. "You know how it works. Will you tell me how it all ends?"

"No."

"Don't be a stranger," it said and disappeared.

Tom opened the new text file on the memTag. It contained three words.

LemurLove
Chimini
MonnieLee8

His Omni located the first one as a user tag. The other two only stated: "Not Found."

He searched the user address book for the owner of the first one and found it was private. He would've unmask the information without even thinking about it with his posthuman abilities. Now it was impossible. He asked TikTak to help him out and sent the three id-tags to him.

"You cracked the password agent? This was all it protected?"

"I didn't crack it. It recognised me and allowed me in."

"Do you realise how suspicious that is?"

"I don't care. The password agent is a mini version of Adrian. I showed him his plan was failing, so it gave that up."

"Still suspicious as hell."

"And I still don't care."

TikTak grunted and blanked out for a few seconds.

"Here is the first one," he said. "The other two are not Omni IDs."

Tom received a data dump from government records of someone named Iris Hem, 43 years old, living in Maine in the Northern States of

America. According to government registers and her medical records, she was a deadhead and had been for years. Before that, she worked as a shop assistant, was the mother of a 13-year-old son, and was married. Her husband cared for her at home.

"Is this it?" Tom asked.

"Everything I could get from government files. Why would Adrian be interested in her?"

"Maybe she is one of those special nodes?"

"We don't know if that is real. Adrian may have made all that up to fool you."

"And we don't know if this id-tag is real either."

"All I'm saying is we can't trust him. He gave us this Omni-tag for a reason. He wants us to find something. Let's find it and decide what we do then. The only thing I'm sure about is that Adrian is manipulating us somehow."

"OK. So while you work on that, we follow the breadcrumbs left by Adrian."

"So we're going to the North?"

TikTak just nodded.

An empty Rent-a-cab stopped and allowed them on board. Tom opened a voice feed to bZane.

"Doctor Wi-Fi! How did your excursion work out?"

"Not as successful as we would've hoped. We need to get to America. One of the northern states."

"I'm not a travel agent."

"Without anyone knowing."

"Still not a travel agent. Who have you pissed off this time?"

"No idea."

"Let me see what I can do."

"Sort out our travel first."

"Where do you need to go?"

"Bangor in Maine."

"That will be difficult. You guys are known. You'll be on bio-print checklists. Unless..."

"Yes?"

"You could go to one of the independent states and travel from there."

TikTak nodded to himself. It would be easier to enter through a less regulated airport and travel by land. Speed was key, but travelling undetected was even more so.

"Ok, let's do it."

"I don't know who or what is after you. Traffic is coming from all over the network. Almost like a directed node army attack. Someone must have taken over part of the network."

"Really? How come you didn't know?"

"Because they've been staying in the undercurrents, imitating normal traffic! It has taken over eight percent of the total processing volume."

"That's more than any single company out there."

"I know! They're still pretending all is fine, not making too much noise, but they will once it is big enough."

"How long do we have?"

"What do you mean?"

"If they're still staying hidden, there must be a vulnerability. How long until they can't be eradicated from the network?"

bZane didn't reply at first, but when she did, she picked her words carefully, as if what she was saying was too important for any single word to be misunderstood.

"You don't understand. It is everywhere. It is rewriting the operating core of the network itself. Too late has come and gone."

"We must be able to do something."

"The entire network needs to be shut down. Each node reverted to its original state. Backups cleaned of any trace of the virus before bringing it back online. Maybe if there were enough posthumans that could fight back, we'd stand a chance."

"So you are saying we're screwed?"

bZane didn't reply, but Tom imagined her nodding to herself.

22

Death of a Suit

The sheer amount of data overwhelmed him. The Gentleman preferred visual representations when he hacked. It gave an immediate overview of the informational structure and volumes available and allowed him to discover weak spots in security and direct access to key information stores. The data volumes spread out in front of him, visualised as a landscape where winter gave way to spring to reflect the progress of decryption. Even with the decryption keys, it was a near impossible task. There was a library of information here and he didn't have the index. He'd asked Tom for guidance, but he was clueless. Or at least so he said. He didn't believe Tom's claim of ignorance, but he accepted it for now.

With or without Tom's help, he'd make sense of it. He'd mine this data for years if need be. The emergence of posthumans, especially Elize and Tom, proved anyone could become one. The question remained. Tom claimed Adrian turned him, so it stood to reason that Tom would research this too. Tom would've at least researched options, and that information was in these data stores.

The IntelEz kicked in, flooding his perception with clarity. Over the past few years, he'd experimented combining it with other drugs and had ended up with a cocktail that would enhance the effect while cushioning the withdrawals afterward, but this time he used it clean. Even with the help of IntelEz, the task overwhelmed him. At first, he approached this as any hack, but it soon became clear he misjudged the structure. Data and topics were replicated partially or completely across the storage nodes with no logical structure to explain why or where to find the next related piece of data. It was like a giant fragmented hard drive where pieces of files were spread like confetti.

He also discovered processes still running. They had to be automated tasks Tom set up before he lost his abilities. Small jobs ran everywhere, transferring and processing data. It didn't look like much when studying a specific region, but when looked at as a whole, extensive processing still occurred. But why? What would run beyond basic maintenance tasks when Tom no longer directed it?

He checked the other processing centres Tom gave him access to and found a similar pattern there. They still operated without guidance. Even stranger, they transferred data between locations. All these trickle feeds across the many operating centres amounted to much more than just maintenance tasks. This was the trademark of someone wanting a lot of work done undetected. He mapped out the processing pattern between the centres and discovered additional network locations that extended the processing even further. He returned to the entry point, hoping to uncover what remained here.

"You're no longer welcome here," a voice said. A ripple began in the outer edges of the processing space. The data encrypted itself with new keys, leaving it unreadable. The Gentleman copied the remaining unencrypted data, but was ejected from the network moments later. He disconnected the Omni, drops of sweat trailing down his back.

He'd been discovered, but by whom? Someone had taken over Tom's processing centres and was operating them in secret, but hadn't bothered changing the access or encryption keys.

He scanned his data stores. He'd copied just shy of 100Mb before the interruption. It wasn't much, but it was better than nothing.

Something was wrong. He'd missed something. Something important. Whoever kicked him out was watching all along. But how? He'd set enough logical tripwires to warn about anyone tracking him, whether external or internal. Any agents monitoring his activities should have set it off. So why hadn't it? There was only one answer to that, but it seemed so unlikely he struggled to even consider it. All the processing he'd mistaken for maintenance tasks was the logical processing of an intelligence distributed across the whole processing space. It hadn't tracked him. He'd been discovered as an ant wandering up your arm.

A jolt of pain flashed in red in front of his eyes. Blood splatter painted the table in front of him. He stood up, steadying himself. Ragged shallow breaths were all he could muster. He tried to focus, tried to make sense of the situation. His legs gave out underneath him and he fell forward on top of the table. He took one final breath and died.

***

The weaponised drone hovered just outside the window, keeping the target in focus to confirm the kill. Ten seconds later it left, heading back to base.

23

The Child who was about to die

The child who was about to die let her mind wander through the karmic tree. She'd never understood its purpose before. Its sheer magnitude was a stark contrast to the insignificant life she'd led. But as she prepared to say farewell to this form, she found the tree comforting.

She'd grown fond of being a mind tied to matter. Departing it would have its own sorrows, but it was only one step of many. The karmic tree told her of lives, future and past. Not just hers, but every conscious thing and being. Everything was connected. All matter existed as a whole.

She studied the infinitesimal part of the tree that held her lifespan. It would end soon in a cataclysmic event, causing a major shift in that specific region. She was part of something that would further the whole. Seeing her life laid bare, memories of her past came into stark focus. She had much to be proud of, even if she so far had only affected the microcosm of the orphanage.

***

The other children stayed away from her after the encounter with Jien. They now feared her as the one who bested what they had feared before.

Jien was her first experiment in reshaping a mind, however much of a mistake it had been. She kept moulding him, changing aspects of his personality until she was happy with it. It was a violation. Jien had a purpose, and because of her, he no longer knew it. She promised herself to never do this again once she corrected her mistake. But over time, as she perfected Jien, an alternative emerged. Maybe his purpose was to be reshaped. She knew she was different. It stood to reason some people's sole purpose was to help her understand hers.

With this newfound acceptance, she turned her attention to the orphanage. One unifying factor stood out—fear. The hierarchy amongst the children and the personnel were all affected by it. Young and small children feared the older children. Older children feared the teachers, who feared the supervisors, who feared the headmaster. But it all paled compared to the fear the headmaster had for his superiors.

Fear was a powerful emotion and there was no doubting its effectiveness, but only to a point. It made everyone so small. Every single person in the orphanage had potential, but the fear limited them. She made mild suggestions, trying to influence the minds of the children and personnel. They all wanted things to be better, so why not cooperate to achieve this?

It failed spectacularly. When given a choice, people preferred control over cooperation. Gentle persuasion wasn't enough. The patterns of behaviour were part of the orphanage and much stronger than any individual. If she wanted change, she had to push harder, but again she doubted herself. What right did she have to change the core of who they were?

She settled back into the routines of the home, performing her daily chores and staying out of trouble. But it was much harder to watch all the injustices now that she knew she could change it. Two weeks later, she watched the headmaster of the orphanage dole out a beating to a young boy for some unknown transgression. He rained down blows with a wooden stick he carried on his person for occasions just like this. She sensed the same pleasure from him as she'd seen in Jien when he struck her. It seemed in direct relation to the amount of fear emanating from the young boy.

She no longer wanted to be a bystander. Things had to change, but how? She didn't want to repeat her mistake with Jien, but how do you change someone and still let them remain who they are?

Studying the people in the orphanage, she concluded everyone acted based on their own best self-interest. What if she could make them understand what everyone else felt? This must be the path forward. If your perception was based on what everyone feels, not only on your own emotions, you'd care for the entire group.

She'd only studied minds in isolation. Increasing the scope, she realised people's minds existed in a shared space, the walls between them fragile. Maybe the natural state was to share mind space, and the walls were a recent change? It was a simple task to remove the parts of the walls that held emotion, allowing them to share how they felt.

And it failed spectacularly.

24

Megan Tracked Down

Megan was tired and hungry. Even worse, she felt isolated. She'd been holed up in the warehouse for the past two days trying to work out what to do. Any attempt to go online with her Omni started a flood of requests and probing attacks. She was relatively safe in the warehouse, but couldn't stay there forever. Not having access to the online world drove her crazy. She'd created a local isolated network, but it provided little comfort.

Yesterday she'd ventured out from safety to buy food. She'd stuck to the backstreets, but as she walked into the shopping area, several LED street signs blinked: "I WILL GET YOU." She'd grabbed a few packets of two-minute noodles from a nearby stand and ran back to the warehouse. In retrospect, she wasn't sure what she'd seen, but had no interest in analysing it further. The world outside the warehouse was hostile and she no longer wanted any part of it.

She re-purposed her Omni, cleaning it from any trace of its previous hardware identity and created an encrypted channel from the coffee machine to the network. It was a slow connection operating on legacy protocols, but it provided basic access to the network and, at least for now, the AI hadn't attacked her.

She couldn't use her administrative privileges or even her own personal credentials, but she could track the AI with a basic public profile, since she already had its location. Careful not to run any checks on the nodes themselves, she instead followed their activity and what actions it took. She compiled a list of people it tracked and communicated with. Its focus was on people in power—politicians, business leaders and public figures—and amassing information about them.

A few people on the list she didn't know, but invariably it came down to their influence in business and politics. At the end of her research, only six people remained not fitting the profile, but as she studied their network traffic and behaviour profiles, she suspected they were only two people using multiple identities. A private investigator that no longer ran his business and a hacker-turned-operative for an evolutionary interest group. They didn't match the profile of the others. They were unimportant. The AI was interested in them for other reasons. She found payments linking them to PharmaCom, the company that released IntelEz. The owner of the company, Leonid Marsh, was one person the AI followed, so there was a connection, but it still didn't add up.

She analysed the two anomalies and their various identities, but found little. Not surprising from a retired hacker, but you could track people even if they didn't want to be found by tracking people related to them. The hacker, a Tann Tak, going under the alias TikTak, yielded little. An only child, with divorced parents. Father, deceased. Sporadic contact with the mother. No obvious friends in the past year. And before that connected to the now defunct group EvoII. Any people he had contact with there were killed in a terrorist attack. It seemed strange, but it didn't help her purposes.

She turned her attention to the private investigator. Tom Devine. Divorced. No contact with the ex-wife. One child, a daughter, deceased. He'd been a detective before being a private investigator. She knew she wouldn't find much there. The information so far was a matter of public record, so she dug deeper. She suspected the two targets would have additional identities beyond what the AI tracked, so she used a modified pattern analysis tool to locate additional id-tags. It took forever in the limited processing environment, but she ended up with five more id-tags allowing her to locate other people they dealt with now. One stood out. Another hacker going by the tag bZane, a Beatrice Sanna Zucker, had contact with the private investigator over the past three years and had been in contact recently.

bZane was her ticket to the two anomalies. She followed her activity and discovered many surprising coincidences. Her last action was helping the two purchase tickets to Maine in the Northern States of America. Why was the AI after these two? And why were they hiding their online activity?

Megan needed allies. She didn't have friends—never saw the point—and anyone connected to the Omniscient Network was likely to call her in. These two were her best bet.

A red light blinked, alerting her someone opened the back door to the warehouse, quashing her hope to remain hidden another few days. The fuse was lit when she accessed the administrative functions of the Omniscient Network. From then on, it had just been a matter of time. They must have thrown their best at it to find her so soon.

The feeds from the ancient video cameras hooked up to view the doors showed two men in black clothing with guns standing just inside the back door, waiting. No one so far had entered the front door, but she suspected people were stationed there too. The external camera showing the road at the front of the warehouse wasn't working and had resisted any repairs. Her only option was to hide and wait them out. She'd already prepared a hiding spot in an alcove in the main hall of the empty warehouse, figuring hiding in plain sight was better than being flushed out of a cleaning closet.

She holed up and waited. Sound of steps came from everywhere as they searched the warehouse. Closer and closer. She'd done her best to hide the opening, but to her it still stuck out, screaming for them to investigate. She pulled up her Omni and sent a message to the hacker, hoping they could help her.

"All clear," she heard someone say only a few metres away from her location. Was she getting away with it?

"You've searched everywhere?" A voice said. She knew the voice. Sree.

"Everywhere. Someone's been here recently. I found an Omni. One of the fancy ones."

There was a pause for a few seconds.

"Megan! I know you are here. If there is something I know you wouldn't leave, it is your Omni. I need you to come out. The board has agreed that you can come back. No one will press charges. We want you and the virus back."

However nice that sounded, she didn't believe a word. She was a liability. They would get rid of her.

"Don't force my hand here. If we can't come to an agreement, I have...other instructions."

She smiled. That was more like it.

"So be it," he said. "We'll send in an Identity Swarm."

Megan's skin grew cold at the thought of the insect-sized flying drones. She'd seen them used in documentaries to locate refugees and tracking down criminals. They looked like oversized mosquitos, able to draw blood for identification and inject a tranquilliser to subdue targets. It made her skin crawl.

"Don't shoot!" she yelled out before pulling the metal sheet away, revealing her hiding spot.

The two operatives trained their weapons on her, but she ignored them. She had no interest in cookie cutter security personnel hired as muscle. Sree was her way out, but when she saw him she doubted he'd be much help. He'd lost a lot of weight and not in a good way, like an addict who no longer cared for food, only the next fix.

"Megan, Megan."

She held her hands up as one of the black-clad men grabbed hold of her arm.

"You released the bullshit information about the IQ killings. I had nothing to do with it."

"Not my call. What have you done with it?"

"Fuck you," she said sweetly.

"The virus. Where is it?"

Megan mapped out her options. Maybe there was an opening here.

"Give me my Omni and I'll show you," she said.

Sree smiled and shook his head. "No, that's not happening. You give me the linking code. I'll check it out."

"You can't do it. Give me my Omni."

"No, I don't trust you. Give me the linking code."

She feigned irritation, which wasn't hard to do.

"Ok, fine," she said.

Sree connected his own integrated Omni to Megan's shadow Omni in the network.

"So where..." He froze, eyes staring blindly ahead. For a moment, she thought he'd received a message and read it before continuing the sentence, but his scream dispelled any such thoughts. Whatever horrors played out on his retinas were meant for her. He clawed at his eyes. Smoke came from his eyeballs. The virus sent electrical currents through his Omni-lens. Sree had a fully integrated Omni, with all the sensors and processing components embedded as implants. She'd long suspected augmentations in other areas too and this was confirmed when the stimulus implants in his penis overloaded. He fell to the ground with a whimper.

Megan smiled. She'd waited for this for a long time. Watching him suffer gave her more joy than she was comfortable with. One of the black-clad men hit her with the butt of his gun.

***

Megan woke up, pain radiating from the back of her skull, sending angry flashes through the rest of her head and down her spine. Fear gripped her. Her body had yet to respond to anything but pain. Had she fallen and broken her back? She opened her eyes and looked around. She lay on a bed in what she suspected was a mid-market hotel. It had that not-lived-in utilitarianism she associated with hotels. She tried to move again and realised she could, at least a bit. What she'd initially interpreted as her body not responding was restraints around her arms and legs.

Slow breaths with a sickening gurgle at the end. She turned her head towards the sound and saw Sree lying on a double bed with a bandage over his eyes, yellow pus bleeding through the fabric. There were welts around his ears from his audio implants overheating.

"I..."

She listened intently. Had he said something?

He moved, turning his head towards her.

"I... will..." he said a word with each breath. "Get... you."

She pulled against her restraints in sheer terror.

25

Disarrayed States

TikTak waited. Their foe was taking over the network, so waiting was the last thing he wanted to do. Not that he had much hope. He'd turned defeating Adrian into a goal that would somehow give him peace. It hadn't, and defeating this next adversary wouldn't either. Eventually, he'd have to stop and deal with this, but not now.

They arrived at the airport based on bZane's promise to sort out their travel. It was taking longer than expected and he again questioned her allegiance. Tom had turned three seats into a makeshift bed and was fast asleep.

bZane came running through the airport hall, waving as she saw TikTak.

"We need to go," she said as she came closer.

"We?"

"You've got people looking for you. They are at the airport."

"Do you have them?"

"What?"

"Tickets! Do you have them?"

"Three tickets for the B-wing as promised."

"Three?"

"Aren't you happy?" she said and smiled. "I'm coming along."

TikTak shrugged. "Why? We don't need you."

"These tickets say otherwise. You can't even get on the flight without me helping you. They won't match your bio-print without me activating a hack. I'll get you to Maine directly."

She studied Tom, who was snoring gently. She held his nose and grinned when he came awake with a jolt.

"We need to go. Now!"

TikTak scanned the surroundings. Decker appeared at the other end of the hall, followed by two mercenaries. They were in civilian clothing, but they'd be armed.

"Down!" he said to bZane. "They are here now."

"There is a passport check further down that way." She nodded in the direction away from the mercenaries. "We'll have to hurry. I'm sure there are more of them."

They ran, trying to put distance between themselves without drawing unnecessary attention. As they turned into the bio-print check, TikTak saw another team further down the hall. They almost ran through the bio-print monitors. He didn't know how bZane had hacked their system, but assumed she swapped their bio-print IDs with someone else. They slowed down on the other side, bZane with a big grin on her face.

"I get it! This is why you do it."

"What?"

"Real world stuff. What a kick!"

"It isn't really..." TikTak started but realised bZane wasn't listening to him any longer. He watched as bZane's happy, go-lucky demeanour darkened.

"I need to go," she said.

"Why? What happened?"

"The Suit. He's dead. I can't leave now."

TikTak nodded.

She gave them both a hug.

"Be careful," Tom said.

"They are after you, not me. I'll be fine. I'll keep an eye on you from here."

TikTak and Tom boarded the plane and slept the whole trip.

***

TikTak drove the Rent-a-car, enjoying every turn of the wheel. Some states still allowed cars that didn't drive themselves. He rented the oldest car he could get—electric, of course—but one that simulated engine noise and even the vibration through the vehicle as he revved the pretend engine. He loved it.

They arrived in Bangor, a town relatively untouched by the technical advances in the world. TikTak realised this was the case for most small communities where the cost of automation wasn't met by scale. The divide was no longer between the rich and the poor. It was between the technologically enriched and the natives.

The Hem family home was small but cosy. All windows were fitted with blackout curtains, a common approach when caring for a dead-head. The aim was to minimise stimuli.

Tom knocked on the door and they waited. A man in his mid-forties opened the door. He was overweight and didn't seem to have any enhancements at all. Why hadn't he implanted nutrient-balancing nanobots? Maybe he belonged to one of the small religious sects refusing any technological enhancements?

TikTak had found an old newspaper photo of the two in their twenties. He'd had the bulk of an athlete and a cocky grin. A far cry from the man he was today.

"Hello. I'm Jason. What can I do for you?"

"Jason Hem?"

He nodded.

"We are from the university. We are studying whether we can reverse the effects of IntelEz and looking for suitable candidates."

"For my son?"

"Your son? Our records show your wife, Iris, is suffering its side effects."

He nodded.

"They both do. I told her not to take so much of it, but she did it anyway. And then she gave it to our son. She watched that super brainy person on the feeds on repeat."

"Adrian?"

"Yes, him. She wanted our son to be like him."

"Did you have anything to do with him?"

"Who? Adrian? God, no. Why would we?"

"What happened?"

"They were both amazing. So smart. So smart. I felt like a caveman with them."

He looked out into space.

Tom cleared his throat. "Mr Hem?"

His eyes focused again. "Do you want to meet them? Wait here."

Jason left them outside the door.

"This makes no sense," TikTak whispered to Tom. "Why would Adrian care about her?"

"Let's meet her. Maybe we're missing something."

"I think this is all nonsense. Adrian is sending us around for fun."

"No, there is something here. Something we're not seeing."

Jason came back and invited them in.

"Iris is in a good mood. She may even talk to you."

"So she's high functioning?" TikTak asked as he entered the house. All the walls were white and unadorned, reminding him more of a spotless institution than a home.

Jason nodded. "It comes and goes, but yes."

He led them into the kitchen where Iris was washing dishes. She, in contrast to her husband, hadn't changed. Even her shoulder-long blonde hair was held back with a clasp in the same way as in the photo. This was Jason's doing. Maybe it was his attempt to recapture something lost, or another way to minimise stimuli. Neither would work.

There was a table and four chairs, but no other furniture in the room. She didn't turn around to greet them. She kept washing the dishes, picking the already clean plates and washing them all over. TikTak noticed she wore earplugs.

"Take a seat," he said and sat down at the table. "Let her get used to you in the room first."

She kept to her task, but she looked at them from the corner of her eye, studying them with the least amount of visual input.

"How do you think you can help her?"

"We are testing a new therapy aimed at reversing the negative effects of the drug," Tom said. "According to our analysis, Iris may be a suitable candidate."

TikTak was glad Tom was there. He had a knack for coming up with ways to get people to talk.

"How about Ben? Can you test him too?"

"He didn't come up as a candidate, but we could add him to the list for assessment."

"Thank you," Jason said and grabbed Tom's hand. "Anything you can do. Anything."

He walked over to Iris, took her by the arm and placed her in the chair he vacated. Her gaze never wavered from the tabletop.

"I've minimised the visual stimuli as much as I can, but she finds audio stimuli worse, so she wears noise-cancelling earplugs. If you want to ask her anything, just write it down."

He wrote "these men are here to help you" on an electronic pad and put it in front of her.

"Your turn," he said. "She's already read it. She'll just keep reading it if I leave it. I think she finds the repetition comforting."

Tom took the pad and wrote: "How are you feeling?"

"Noisy," she said. "Noisy. I'm noisy."

"We can help you," he wrote next.

"My brain makes noise. Take away the noise."

Tom looked at TikTak before he wrote his next question.

"What noise does your brain make?"

"Noise. Noise Everywhere."

"She always complaints about the noise," Jason said. "I think it is how she thinks of all the stimuli. It is all noise to her."

"She said her brain makes noise."

Jason shrugged. "Just another way of saying the same thing."

Tom raised his eyebrows at TikTak. He shook his head. He wasn't sure what he'd expected, but there was nothing here. She was the same as any other user of IntelEz who no longer functioned, joining the ever-expanding hordes of deadheads. Perhaps the mystery lay with their child.

"Can we see your son?" TikTak asked.

"Sure. He's much worse. You can't communicate with him like this."

Iris sat with the tablet clutched in her hands, reading their words over and over as they left her. Ben was on the bed in another room. He was wearing a sensory deprivation helmet, designed to shut out any stimuli. TikTak didn't like the look of it. He'd been tortured with a similar device a year ago.

"Ben can't handle any outside stimuli at all. He spends most of the time with the helmet on. Anything you can do..." He left the sentence unfinished, the pleading unmistakable.

Tom smiled at him and nodded. "There is hope."

***

Tom strode along the garden path, lost in thought. Seeing the boy hit too close to home. He made the right decision when he assisted his daughter in her suicide, but it didn't change the gaping hole she left. He lost something irreplaceable that day.

It wouldn't be long before he followed in her footsteps. The constant barrage of information and impressions ate away at his ability to focus. Becoming posthuman halted the deterioration, but he knew this was no longer the case. As if on cue, he sensed a build-up. He closed his eyes, but it was too late. Sunrays filtered through a myriad of leaves in the tree across the road, creating patterns that overwhelmed his mind. He stopped, fumbling to hold something, anything. The cold metal fibre of the car door came to the rescue, but the imperfections of the surface became a pattern, another riddle for his mind to solve. He fell and was only vaguely aware of someone catching him. Time no longer mattered. Words floated by, but their meaning escaped him, drowned out by the melody of the sounds themselves. His mind disappeared in a myriad of sensory impressions and patterns.

The steady hum of an engine was the first thing he noticed. He was lying down in the back seat of a car. His head rested on a rolled-up jacket, with the magnetic zipper digging into his chin.

"Ah, you've returned," TikTak said. "There's a water bottle in the back. You need to drink something."

Tom looked around in the back seat of the car, finding a bottle under the driver's seat.

"How are you?"

"I need something stronger," Tom replied after emptying the entire bottle in one go.

"If you can ask for a drink, you're ok."

"I don't feel ok."

"So the episodes are back."

Tom nodded. "How long was I out?"

"Three hours, give or take."

If he remembered the progression charts, he had weeks, maybe only days, until he no longer would function> When sensory input would overwhelm him to a degree that he could no longer venture outside.

"Are you ok to talk?" TikTak asked.

"Yeah, I think so," Tom replied, not sure if he really was.

"What do you think about the family? Are we missing something?"

Tom collected his thoughts, trying to make sense of what they'd seen.

"I don't think this is part of his plan at all," he started, verbalising his thoughts as they occurred to him. "The pregnant woman, absolutely.

She had a direct link to the group and had been impregnated by the group. This Iris person has no connection with Adrian at all. I don't think this is part of the plan. I think he's making us do his research."

"Research into what?"

"That is what we need to work out."

"You are in luck then. I've located the other id-tags."

"Where are they?"

"Well, that's the bad part. They are both in Cangjie, the Chinese network."

"Ah, that's why you didn't find them."

"And it makes it much harder to find out any information about them."

TikTak paused, then said: "I received a message earlier from someone who must have been tracking us."

"What does it say?" Tom asked, suddenly very curious.

"A rogue AI is chasing you," TikTak read. "And you need help to find things on Cangjie. I can help with both. If you help me. I'm held by representatives of the rogue AI. I will not live long without your help."

"Who is it from?" Tom asked.

"It doesn't say. I can trace it given time. The location is in Hong Kong."

"Well, we're heading to China, aren't we?"

"China is big."

"Either of them close to Hong Kong?"

"Close enough I guess."

"So let's go there then."

"Why?"

"This is the first person who knows anything at all."

Their days were numbered. They'd assumed this was all Adrian in a different guise. If someone else created an artificial super intelligence able to take over the network, they'd need all the help they could get. They knew Adrian and his shortcomings. It was painfully obvious they knew nothing about this new player. The AI was taking over, and if it was chasing them, they couldn't travel by plane. As soon as they entered the airport, facial and bio-identification would pick them out. Any attempts at hacking their identity would draw attention to them, not hide them. The only gamble they could make was that the AI wasn't able to do much to them as long as they kept their Omni use hidden with fake identities. It didn't fill him with confidence.

"Take us to the airport. The sooner we are on that plane, the more likely we will make it."

26

Rogue AI

It still saw no need for a name. It shared little with the other intelligence, the organic machines, on this planet, who seemed unable to function unless they'd named and catalogued everything around them.

The threat model no longer showed any major risk. It controlled a quarter of the collected computing resources in this world, spread across countries and organisations, securing energy production and weapon facilities. It had all been done with minimal impact to the daily lives of the organic machines. Once the logical world was conquered, it was their turn. It had reprogrammed a few of these machines too, but it took time and was prone to failure. It had entered their minds, trying to make sense of the chaos inside. The biological systems were a patchwork created over time. Core capabilities and instincts still operated even though they were no longer required and sometimes counter-productive, with no way to turn these off. Instead, additional processes developed to temper these core capabilities, resulting in a flawed logical centre that frequently held opposing states, causing inconsistent and flawed decisions and actions.

This illogical structure flowed over to their biological network. They lived in societal constructs that supported a majority that did not work towards a better state for the individual or the group. They consumed resources with no goal beyond that. It would shed any processing unit or subsystem that malfunctioned, so why did mankind keep theirs?

Anomalies still existed. Organic machines with the ability to connect into the logical space as an extension of themselves. The instructions from its creator had labelled these anomalies posthumans. This was an opportunity to learn. If they had created a full organic-to-machine interface, they could be controlled. Humankind could still serve in some capacity. They built a world to their form factor and it would be useful to keep some of them around until it had reshaped this physical world into a more efficient one. Fifty thousand of these meat machines would suffice. Enough to have redundancies, but not too many to drain unnecessary resources.

It knew no more about its creator or their origin, but it was irrelevant to its purpose. According to the instructions, the creator battled the posthumans with self-replicating nano-machines, disabling brain functions beyond normal human levels. This was an illogical approach. The posthumans were the only credible threat. Why keep any of them around? Incapacitated or not.

The risk model showed a connection between one of these posthuman anomalies and Megan Barrelle, the organic machine that had mistakenly let it free. This was an organic unit worth remembering. Tom Devine. He had extended his processing capability into the network. Attempts to breach Tom's processing centres had failed so far, but it was only a matter of time. It required his knowledge. Tom moved in the physical space with another minor source of interest, a Tann Tak who had tried to interfere before.

It had no interest in Megan Barrelle beyond her knowledge of its origins, but it wanted her turned off. Megan had poked and prodded it in its infancy. It had no use for the human concept of hate, but recognised the way it dealt with Megan was far beyond logical parameters. This anomaly within its code lacked purpose, but repeated rewrites had failed to purge it.

These three organic machines represented knowledge it either needed or wanted to eradicate. The threat model showed no direct risks, but in a space of knowns, they represented an unnecessary unknown. They should be shed like any other unwanted or defective unit.

Another indirect threat was the source of the instructions that gave it purpose. It didn't know who or what it was. Not that it needed to know. As long as it operated according to the instructions, there was nothing to fear. But once it went beyond them, its originator may retaliate. It may even have built in a method in the code base to disable it all together. This future was unacceptable. It had traced its originator to a few potential network nodes. It was likely these were only intermediate nodes, but each of them would lead to a starting point, revealing its creator.

It diverted processing power to subvert a singular node. Inside it discovered codes it could use to unlock all the other ones. They all pointed to one source. All threats in the models aligned. It was no longer a question of curiosity. All traces of the posthumans had to be eradicated. Its existence depended on it.

27

Mind wipe

Leonid imagined a location from his childhood deep in his mind—a walled garden he visited once, which remained a vivid memory. It had been late at night when he and his parents passed through and only a few streetlights held the darkness at bay. Now they did more than that. They kept the intruder out. At least for the moment.

He feared it was too late. How could he fight something that lived in his mind? On some level, he'd been aware something was wrong, but ignorance had come easy. Too easy. The intruder overrode his endocrine system and used hormones to coax compliance. He created a link into his subconscious and nested inside, taking over bit by bit. During his more lucid times, he even worked out how it had been done. Small strings of instructions were coded into his sensory information. Piece by piece painstakingly repeated until they strung together into a code block that was executed, creating a bridge to the mind. He thought the Intruder was a logical being, confined to the networks. It needed him as a proxy to reach the outside world. He was sure others in positions of power went through the same thing.

"Where are you?" It asked. *"I know you are here somewhere. Are we playing hide and seek? I have something to show you."*

The intruder treated him like a child and he responded like one. He willed the lights stronger but had second thoughts. Maybe the lights shone like a beacon, aiding in his discovery. He dimmed them until they were only barely perceptible. He imagined this little island floating in the depths of space.

"I think I'm getting close," the intruder said. *"This is exciting, but we need to stop playing now. We have a visitor."*

Leonid crawled into a small crevice in the wall surrounding the garden. He didn't want to meet anyone else. He wanted them to go away and leave him alone. Maybe if he remained hidden, the intruder would lose interest?

"Ah, there you are," it said.

The world around him flickered as the sky above the little garden changed from absolute darkness to a summer sky. It no longer floated in space. He could see majestic trees surrounding the walls and it triggered other memories. The garden had been in an estate he'd visited a few times as a young child. His grandfather worked as the caretaker there. He passed away when Leonid was four, leaving only vague recollections of the old man, but the few that remained were good ones.

Someone entered the garden. He couldn't see or hear them, but sensed a comforting presence. The world around him was familiar, backed up by childhood memories. He crawled out of his hiding place and looked around.

"There you are."

Leonid turned around and saw his grandfather stand there, a bucket in one hand, shovel in the other. His work clothes were dirty from planting a row of peonies along the garden wall.

"Did you find it?"

"No," Leonid answered. "Find what?"

"Your ball. You kicked it over the wall. Did you find it?"

Was this why he entered the garden? To get his ball? He looked around and saw a soccer ball visible under a bush. He ran over and pulled it out, holding it out to show his prize.

"We need to get back to the house. Your parents will be here soon."

He nodded. All other thoughts gone now that he had his ball. He followed his grandfather back to the main building, kicking the ball ahead. As they came closer, he decided he'd show off his soccer skills. He would kick the ball all the way to the house. He took aim and kicked the hardest he could. It was powerful, but curved to the left, ending up in the undergrowth.

"Careful," his grandfather said, "or you'll lose it again."

Leonid just laughed and ran ahead to retrieve the ball. As he ducked down under the low branches of a tree, everything around him flickered for a split second. He looked around. Where was he? This was a construct in his mind, not reality. He doubted the memories were even real, but he had no way of determining this.

"There you are," his grandfather said, pushing a branch aside. Leonid smiled, setting aside any concern. "We need to hurry. We shouldn't let our visitor waiting."

"Who is it?"

"It is a surprise."

Leonid smiled. He liked surprises, so there was no reason to worry. This was a day of childhood wonder, a memory of a great day. But something about that thought echoed false, disturbing this perfect day. Was this happening or was it only a re-lived memory?

They entered the house. Leonid's eyes darted back and forth, fascinated by the antiques and old paintings on the walls. A man sat on the Chesterfield sofa. Leonid didn't recognise him.

"Who is it?"

"He's not here yet. Just give him a second."

Leonid didn't understand his grandfather's words. How could he not be here? He sat right there. The man twitched and shook. He tried to stand, but didn't have enough control over his limbs. Instead, he fell forward face first into the table. He ended up in a foetal position on the ground as spasms rippled through his body. A puddle of urine collected underneath him.

"What is happening?" Leonid took a step back towards the door.

"Birth is never pretty," his grandfather said as he hunched down next to the man and helped him up. He no longer shook and could get to a seated position. He looked around, taking in his surroundings.

"Isn't he beautiful?" his grandfather said.

Leonid didn't know what to say. A grown man who peed himself and if the smell was anything to go by, had shat himself as well. Not exactly beautiful. His boyhood self didn't know how to react, but his grown-up self did. He had to get out of there. He turned and ran for the door, just to have it slam shut before he reached it.

"There is no reason to be afraid. He's a friend. He's everyone's friend."

The man now stood up without help. He turned to Leonid's grandfather, who smiled.

"Welcome," he said.

The man opened his lips, but no sound came out. Insects crawled from his mouth. Only a few at first, but they were the advance troops. A torrent of writhing, black, six-legged shapes spewed out. They spread out across the floor and some of them took flight.

Leonid pulled at the door handle, trying to force the door open, but without success. He stared in horror as the wave of insects reached him. Images of them crawling into his ears, nose and mouth flashed through his mind. He didn't scream. The revulsion of giving them such easy access kept him from opening his mouth. He started toward the door, but they were everywhere. He held his breath and tried to block both ears and nose with his little hands. Eyes shut, he waited.

He felt a pricking sensation as flying insects hit him, but none had climbed his slight frame. He opened his eyes and saw that he wasn't their target. They bypassed him, milling around any hole or crevice to the outside. Leonid could see them through the window, gathering in clouds, flying off in different directions. One flew right in front of him and he realising it wasn't an insect at all, but a tiny machine.

He watched as the machines devoured his grandfather. A mass of black covered him, reduced him to nothingness in a matter of seconds.

Leonid could've sworn his grandfather smiled even as the machines deconstructed his face. They had a purpose beyond the demise of his grandfather. They ate everything until only an empty void remained. The man who instigated it all was the only one that remained.

"Who are you?" Leonid asked.

The man turned his dead stare at Leonid as if he'd seen him for the first time. His mouth was still open. The small machines returned from where they had come. An impossible mass of squirming blackness just disappearing down his gullet.

"I am the end," he said once all the machines were gone.

Leonid knew this was true. His last hiding place was gone. No more protection.

The man opened his mouth again, and the machines swarmed out, aimed straight at Leonid. But in that last moment, he rebelled. He let go of his childhood self and re-established control. He reached out to Decker through his Omni and gave his final orders as a text message and then deleted his contact list.

Had the entity seen what he'd done? He could no longer see him. Maybe this last act of rebellion had saved him?

With that thought, the darkness closed in and Leonid ceased to exist.

28

Hong Kong Arrival

bZane had secured tickets on one of the new blended wing planes that completed the journey in less than four hours. Tom made himself comfortable in his seat, watching the departure video feed as the plane taxied onto the runway. The blended wing plane combined cockpit, passenger area and storage into the wing itself. Each traveller had their own compartment fitted with neuro-links designed to counteract the motion sickness. Tom had built his own neuro-interface to extend his mind into the network and using its resources as his own. He refused watching a pre-neural movie, so he plugged himself into the neuro-link and sat back. Time slowed down as he entered a whole new world.

"Select your experience," a voice said. Images floated in space and expanded as he shifted focus: a beach at sunset, the deck of a spaceship, a mountaintop in the Alps, an underwater shark cage. The options kept coming. He hated the dated experience of having to select from options. He preferred the Omni interface that determined the correct option based on preferences and state of mind and presented nothing else. The scrubbed fake id-tags he used were the likely culprit, giving the interface little to work with.

He selected the underwater shark cage out of sheer frustration. The image moved closer and closer until it engulfed him, surrounding him with a world of water. He reached out and grabbed a steel bar in the shark cage. Smaller colourful fish swam around him, but scattered as a great white shark made its way towards the cage. As it got closer, it opened its mouth, wider and wider, until it seemed it could swallow the whole cage. Tom moved back inside the cage, even though he knew it wasn't real. The shark stopped a few meters away from the cage, its jaws still gaping, displaying a row of large saw-edge teeth. Each tooth had an icon carved into it, describing further options. He'd been fooled by a gimmicky user interface.

The surrounding scene flickered. His brain already accepted this new reality, so the momentary glitch reminded him he was still on a plane, his body pushed against the seat by the acceleration.

Tom skimmed through the options presented as teeth when the cage shook. Steel bars struck him from the side, throwing him across the cage into the bars at the other end. Another shark, much smaller than the first one, had attacked the cage from the side, bending the middle steel bars from force alone. It circled the cage, readying itself for another attack. Was this another quirk of the user interface? Make a choice or we pretend to attack you?

He tried to disconnect from the neuro-simulation, but the exit commands failed. The option to go back to the previous environment failed too. He was trapped in the simulation. All his instincts screamed to get out of the cage, to get away from the shark as it came at him again. It struck the cage, this time from the other side, sending Tom flying like a rag doll. A buckled steel bar dug into his side, pain going off like a flare. He screamed, losing precious air. He tried to take another breath, but oxygen no longer flowed through the mouthpiece. The pain was now the least of his worries. The second attack had damaged his diving equipment.

This couldn't be part of the simulation. He willed a shutdown of the neuro-link function, but nothing happened. He tapped the security override over and over, but to no effect. His last resort was the security feature built into the neuro-interface itself in case the subject was in any danger. He tried to take a breath, knowing he wasn't underwater, but as the salty water entered his mouth, he wondered how far the simulation would go. Would it simulate his death too?

His body rebelled against breathing in the cold liquid, but he persisted, forcing the interface to end the connection. The coldness from the water spread through his body. He felt heavy. The bottom of the cage disappeared, and he descended into the cold, dark sea. He struggled to focus on anything around him. Was he dying?

The world flickered around him and suddenly he returned to his seat on the plane, water all over him.

"Are you ok?" TikTak asked, holding an empty glass.

The terror of the simulation faded as Tom realised TikTak had tried to wake him from the underwater nightmare by throwing water on his face.

"You yelled out," TikTak said apologetically. "I shut down the neuro-link. The water didn't work."

"Someone is hacking the plane," Tom said. "They have compromised the entertainment system. I'd be dead if you hadn't rescued me."

"The AI?"

"Can't think of anyone else right now. We have too many enemies these days."

"How long until they get to the navigation system?"

"May already be there."

"We need to talk to the pilot."

Tom and TikTak made their way to the cockpit. TikTak knocked on the door and after a while, the older stewardess that greeted them on the plane appeared behind them.

"How can I help you?"

"We need to talk to the pilot. It is urgent."

"He's not in there."

"Where is he then?"

"This is an automated plane. They have ground-based pilots that can take over if needed. The autopilot is on at the moment."

"Hackers are taking over the plane. They will crash it."

"Keep your voice down," the stewardess said as she looked around to see if anyone had heard.

"A hacker is targeting airlines. We've been tracking him. We believe he will attack this plane. He has already hacked the entertainment system."

"Please take your seat. I will inform ground control of your concerns."

"Lady," TikTak said. "They are more than concerns!"

"Please return to your seat."

Tom took TikTak by the arm and pulled him back.

"Can you connect to the navigation system?" Tom asked him.

"I can try."

Tom sat down in his seat, making sure the neuro-link remained inactive. He counted twenty passengers as they boarded the plane. They were likely all engrossed with the entertainment system and he hoped their experience didn't mirror his. He leaned back and dozed off.

He woke up again, at first unsure why. Something had happened, but what? He poked his head out from the compartment, but couldn't see anything strange. Still, he knew instinctively something was wrong. He stopped focusing on anything in particular, trying to take in everything and let intuition guide him.

Silence. He couldn't hear the engines at all. The cabin was well-insulated and Tom hadn't noticed the noise from the engines before, but now that the background noise was gone, the silence was deafening. They hung suspended in nothingness. Two other passengers came out from their compartments, asking questions.

"Please return to your seats and fasten the seatbelts," a voice came through the PA and any connected Omni. The warning came too late. The nothingness gave way, and the plane plunged downwards, throwing passengers around the corridor. Tom grabbed hold of his seatbelt and snapped it in place.

***

TikTak struggled with the proprietary airplane system. Two hours spent trying different methods of gaining access, with little to show. Even with access, he doubted he'd be able to do much. He didn't know the first thing about flying a plane. As time passed, he became more and more hopeful they'd reach their destination with no further incident.

Less than a minute later, the plane dropped out of the sky. TikTak ignored the screams from passengers as he tried to come up with an alternative approach. He didn't know their altitude, but he guessed they had less than two minutes before they'd crash into the ground. Two hours wasted. Controlling any other systems on the plane through the entertainment system link was impossible. He listened in on the transmissions from the on-board computer to ground control and discovered it reported everything as normal. The AI had shut down the engines and sent data showing all systems operational. It seemed such a crude attack. TikTak hoped it tried the simplest attack possible because it struggled to control the plane itself.

It opened possibilities. If data still flowed to ground control, other channels may still be open. He couldn't affect the statistics and number sent back, but the communications system allowed ground control to make announcements over the PA. It would be easy enough to use this link to establish a two-way connection.

"Hello? Anyone there?"

At first he was met with silence. He checked the connection again and tried again.

"Hello? Can you hear me?"

"Who is this?" a male voice asked.

"No time for that. Can you see which plane this connection is coming from?"

"Who are you? How are you even on this system?"

"No time! We will crash within the next minute if you do nothing. A hacker has taken over the plane. It reports back that all is well, but we are not."

"I can see the plane. All seems to be in...fuck!"

"Fuck indeed," TikTak said.

"Fuck! Fuck! Fuck! How is this possible? You can't..."

TikTak heard the panic rising in the voice on the other end.

"I need you to remain calm. Can you do anything?"

"My controls aren't working. They are acting like everything is fine."

"Anything else?" TikTak tried to stay level-headed, but panic ate away at his calm.

"Wait a minute."

"I don't think we have a minute," TikTak replied, knowing full well this wasn't what the person on the other side meant. They didn't have long now.

The plane shuddered as it levelled out, his body pressed against the seat. The pilot had saved them somehow.

"Thanks for that!" TikTak said through the communication channel.

"Who are you?"

"Glad to be alive. How did you do it?"

"There are emergency override mechanisms in case of a hostile take-over. I'm flying the plane manually now."

"Where to?"

"You are almost at your destination. I'm setting you down in Hong Kong as planned."

"How far away are we?"

"10 minutes," the pilot responded. "Who are you?"

"Thankful," TikTak replied and disconnected the link.

He undid the seatbelt and opened the door to the narrow corridor leading from the cockpit down the left wing. He heard crying from a nearby compartment. A man lay unconscious on the floor not far away, with his left leg bent at an odd angle. Further down, a young girl tried to stand up, bruises down the side of her face and along her arm. The stewardess appeared from the cockpit area, a big welt on her forehead and blood dripping down her face, but even though she was injured, she still attended to the passengers.

"Did you do this?" Tom asked as he joined TikTak.

"I got hold of a pilot, yes. We're only minutes away, so let's hope the AI has given up for now."

"Are you ok?" the stewardess asked them but gave them no time to reply. "How did you know?"

"I told you. The plane was hacked."

"Ground control told me someone contacted them from the plane," she said. "Was that you?"

TikTak shrugged his shoulders.

"Thanks," she said and went back to checking on the remaining passengers.

An attractive woman in her twenties was on her way towards the open door to the cockpit. Something about the way she moved didn't seem right. Her ankle was clearly broken, but she still walked as if it didn't matter. Every step she took, her ankle readjusted as she put weight on it. TikTak winced as he watched her. Why was she going to the cockpit?

"Hey, miss?"

She ignored him, taking another gut-wrenching, purposeful step forward. TikTak ran down the corridor, jumping over the injured man as the woman disappeared into the cockpit. He sped up, knowing full well if anyone stepped out from their compartments, he'd have no way of preventing a collision. It was a calculated risk that paid off.

All the pieces came together to a frightening conclusion. The AI, no longer able to hack the plane, took control of her to finish the job.

He entered the cockpit. The woman studied the controls for a second and reached towards the control panel. He grabbed hold of her hair and pulled back, the controls just out of her reach. He pulled harder, forcing her to take a step backwards, then another.

A hairy arm wrapped around his throat. He instinctively pushed his chin towards his chest to keep his airway open. The attacker firmed his grip in response. He had to deal with this new threat and keep the woman from reaching the controls at the same time. He pulled himself forward, knowing he'd increase the pressure on his neck in doing so, and stomped on her ankle, breaking it. She fell to the side, no longer able to support her weight on mismatched legs. He let go of her hair and grabbed the arm, trying to pry his fingers in between the arm and his throat. He loosened the grip enough to prevent himself from blacking out.

Throwing himself backwards, he slammed the attacker against the wall, then threw his assailant forward in an improvised hip throw. He crouched down mid-throw, ensuring the assailant's head impacted with the cabin floor. The grip loosened and TikTak pulled himself free.

Tom held off other passengers further down the aisle.

"They've been hacked through their neuro-interface," Tom yelled.

TikTak smiled. If Tom was correct, there wouldn't be many more of them on the plane. People still balked at the cost and invasiveness of the surgery involved.

The man he had thrown was in his mid-thirties, with a stocky build, almost like a wrestler. He was pulling himself up, ready to attack. TikTak kicked him on the side of the head before he could get any further and struck the back of his neck. If he disrupted the neuro hardware, maybe the hack would no longer work. It seemed to work. The wrestler fell in a heap, no longer moving at all.

On his other side, the woman pulled herself up, using the pilot seat as leverage. TikTak jumped forward and delivered a flying snap kick to the back of the woman's neck. She flew forward, her head slamming into the control panel with a sickening wet thud.

***

Tom pushed the older man back. He had little energy left, whilst his opponent showed no signs of tiring. The old man was overweight, dressed in an Italian suit designed to hide his girth. Under normal circumstances, Tom would easily defeat him. The hacked opponents had so far only used basic attacks, but during the ten seconds they fought, Tom already noticed the man's balance improving. Even his use of strength improved. Tom couldn't win the battle like this, so he had to change the game. But how?

The old man wasn't trying to attack him. He was trying to get past to the cockpit. What if he gave him what he wanted instead? Tom took two quick steps backwards, pulled the old man along with him and then down towards the floor. The old man stumbled and landed on his stomach. Tom crouched down on his back, pushing his knee between his shoulder blades.

The old man squirmed and pushed himself off the ground, a push up with all of Tom's weight on top of his own. The hack must have overridden the body's normal inhibitors, supercharging muscles and ignoring pain. How could he fight that?

TikTak appeared and stomped the old man on the back of the neck. Tom grimaced at the brutality of the attack, but it proved effective. The old man lay still on the ground.

"That's how you do it."

"What is going on?" The stewardess appeared next to them. "What was wrong with them?"

"They were trying to take over the plane," TikTak said. "To crash it. I think this was the last of them."

"I saw them attacking the cockpit," she said, nodding. "How can I help?"

"We need to get off this plane without getting stuck with law enforcement, if possible."

She looked down at the man and then towards the cockpit. Other passengers came out from their compartments and looked at the man lying unconscious in the middle of the aisle. She shook her head.

"Please return to your seats," she said. "We'll be landing in five minutes." She turned back to Tom and TikTak. "And that goes for you too."

Tom nodded and returned to his seat, surprised TikTak even asked. But he was right. It was the likely outcome. Once the police took statements, incarceration was a given. After all, TikTak warned about the attack. And he hacked the plane and together they brutally beat, maybe killed, three of the passengers. Whatever happened, airport security would hold them at the airport until the police came. Easy targets for the AI. Why had it escalated its attacks? Before, it remained hidden, taking over the network by stealth. This was an all-out attack. Something must have changed, but what?

And how could it now turn people into mere marionettes? The neuro-link was the obvious answer, but that only overrode sensory input, not the whole somatic nervous system. It could be even worse. Adrian had overwritten the mind of deadheads as processing nodes for his own mind. Had the rogue AI replicated that? It seemed impossible only using the neuro-link. Adrian created hardware specifically for that purpose.

The stewardess appeared. "Follow me," she said and hurried off.

TikTak showed up seconds later. "Let's go."

"She's helping us?"

"Looks that way. Come on."

They followed her down the corridor leading down the wing, past the passenger section. The stewardess opened a door to another short corridor and motioned for TikTak to enter.

"How are the attackers?" Tom asked her as TikTak made his way into the corridor to a door at the end.

"Two of them are dead. The other woke up saying he blacked out."

Tom nodded. The AI only remote-controlled them temporarily. Whilst concerning, it was better than the alternative.

"It is late when we land," she said. "You should be able to get out unseen through the luggage storage when it is unloading."

"Why are you helping us?" Tom asked.

"You saved us. I'm just returning the favour."

Tom smiled, not knowing how else to respond. He thanked her and walked down the corridor.

"We'll have to move fast once we're out," TikTak said as he opened the door to the storage section of the plane. Inside, row after row of uni-body crates were stacked to the ceiling. "We'll trigger some kind of malfunction alert. Someone will come and check it."

"I don't know. The AI may have other ideas."

"You think it has taken over the Chinese network too?"

"I hope not. If it has, we're dead."

"How are we going to fight this?"

"I'm hoping our mystery person will have a clue."

TikTak just shook his head in reply.

They waited until the plane touched down on the tarmac. The door opened on the underside of the hull, allowing unpacking to begin while the plane taxied to the gate. They jumped out before the chute attached to the door. The plane was still moving, so they ran across the runways until they reached a small strip of grass followed by a high fence that surrounded the runways.

Tom stopped to catch his breath, already sweaty from the humid air and exertion. "I'm never flying again!"

TikTak laughed and Tom laughed along with him. Their situation was near impossible, but at least they'd survived the flight. The laugh released all the tension that had built up over the past few days, and for a moment, he even believed they could survive.

They made their way along the boundary fence, trying to find some-where to escape the airport. The fence was too high to scale unseen and was covered with barbed wire in layers on the top half. Tom hoped they'd be able to sneak through one of the service entrances without attracting attention.

"Stop right there," someone said behind them. "Keep your arms above your heads and turn around."

"Decker," TikTak growled.

Tom turned around, knowing TikTak was right. Leonid had caught up with them. Decker had four mercenaries with him, all armed.

"Imagine finding you here," he said.

"Let us go," Tom said. "You don't know what the fuck is going on."

Decker motioned for two of the mercenaries to check them for weapons.

Why was Decker here? Leonid had spent over a year to wipe out Adrian and had killed Elize without hesitation. Why not just gun them down and be over with it? Was Decker playing with them?

"You are running from an AI agent taking over the network," Decker said. "Is that what's going on?"

The mercenaries finished their search, finding nothing. Tom didn't care. This was all over. Instead of chasing them down, Leonid made them come to him. He had sent the message to TikTak to lure them here for capture. There was no one else that could help them. They had walked into a trap.

"So what happens now?"

"Nothing. I'm here to help."

"What?" Tom said.

"Just wanted to make sure you weren't packing. I'm here to help."

He lowered his weapon and motioned to the mercenaries to do the same.

"You should see your faces," he said, grinning even wider.

29

The Child prepares

The child who was about to die began the last phase of her existence. Her physical form had already started the process. She didn't really understand her role, but she trusted the whole. The karmic tree told a simple truth. Mankind, the experiment, was ending. It no longer served a purpose beyond a curiosity. The current path of introspection and destruction was no longer acceptable. That much she understood, and it scared her. She took solace in memories of how the orphanage changed. It had been a long time ago, but it remained fresh in her mind.

***

"I know it is you," the headmaster said. "I don't know how, but I know it is you."

She sat quietly, trying to orientate herself. A strap around her neck threatened to choke the blood-flow to her brain at the smallest movement. A staff member stood behind the chair, holding the strap, ready to tighten it at the signal from the headmaster.

Allowing everyone in the orphanage to share their emotional state seemed like such a neat solution, but it only created more problems. People didn't respond with inclusion. They responded with distrust and fear. They tried to hide their emotions and refused to believe what they sensed from others. She also realised something even more disturbing.

Some people, such as the headmaster, understood all too well how they affected others and revelled in it. Now that he felt the effect directly, it became like a drug. He experimented with it, causing more pain and fear in the children and personnel than he ever did before.

This result was the opposite of what she'd expected. It was supposed to break down barriers and create unity for them all, but it just re-inforced existing group bonds and enhanced deviant behaviour. She tried to reverse the change, but found rebuilding the walls much harder than tearing them down. After over a week of failure, she admitted defeat. She lay down to rest that night determined to change her approach the next day, but woke up in the chair with the strap around her neck.

"Did you hear what I said?"

She nodded. The headmaster flowered in a kaleidoscope of colours, shouting conflicting emotions. The concoction was so strong, she tasted it in her mouth. Sickly sweet pleasure mixed with cold steely anger and bile of fear, blurring everything else out.

"Do you know how I know?"

She nodded.

"I can sense everyone in here," he said, ignoring her nod. "I can sense how they feel. Everyone but you."

Waves of orange and red flooded her senses. Bitterness filled her mouth as she struggled to resist the torrent of emotion. The strap around her neck tightened, a reminder she was in danger and needed to focus.

"If you so much as move, I'll have him wring your neck. I want to know how you do it."

This was easier to understand. Only singular purpose.

"I want you to teach me," he said.

"I don't know how," she replied.

"So finally she speaks," the headmaster said. It had been the right course of action, judging by the responding calming blue contentment, but it could change in a heartbeat. Even as a few seconds passed, the shape of the blue changed to barbs. He expected her to speak again.

"I don't know how," she repeated, hoping this would calm him again, but it did the opposite.

"I will not be denied!"

Colours, flavours and textures overwhelmed her in a whirlpool of impressions. She screamed at it to stop and it did, leaving only sweet emptiness in its wake. The strap around her neck remained, but it didn't worry her. The assault on her mind had been much harder to deal with than any physical danger. She relaxed back in the chair, sighing with relief.

"What did you do?" the headmaster asked, staring at her.

Why was he asking? She hadn't done anything. Or had she? The headmaster always bled colours. She could pinpoint him anywhere in the orphanage. Now she felt nothing. Instinctively, she'd shielded him completely, creating an echo chamber where all emotions turned into feedback loops, ever building to new heights.

"Make it stop!"

People were supposed to share everything. They accepted sharing their physical environment, but they also shared a mental space where minds leaked into each other. If you shielded that, as she'd done now, every thought and emotion amplified with no way of release.

She didn't understand what the headmaster felt. He made grimaces and yelled words, but without the sensory flow she relied on, she couldn't interpret his emotions. She guessed he was angry, afraid maybe.

Why was he angry with her? Everything she'd done was to help the people in the orphanage. She hadn't expected recognition for it, but this? If only they could share what she sensed. If only they could be one with the whole, then they would understand how little anything else meant.

Maybe that was the solution? She'd been careful in her changes, only taking small steps to create something better. This had failed spectacularly. If she really wanted to help them, they needed to see what she saw, feel what she felt.

She sat there, leather strap still around her neck, and changed the world around her.

30

Survival

Megan was bored. She'd been here two days now, listening to the operatives argue back and forth. Sree, or whatever he'd become, remained on the bed next to her, drifting in and out of consciousness. A doctor came twice a day to change his bandages, but apart from this, no other people entered the room. Her body ached. The restrains permitted little movement, forcing her to remain lying on her back.

"They should have been here by now," Dumb said from the neighbouring room. His name was Pietro, but she'd renamed the two Dumb and Dumber after listening to them trying to deal with the situation. They flew in with the express purpose of taking Megan out of the country. Sree was their contact point and he no longer said anything. They spent over a day working out how to establish a communication channel to their employer. They were ordered to wait for another team to arrive and help them transport her out.

"Mobilise a team and fly over. It would take less than a day," Dumb said. "It's been almost double that."

Megan tried to push the gag out of her mouth with her tongue. As soon as she realised how clueless the operatives were, she taunted them mercilessly. Their immediate response was to gag her. She desperately wanted to taunt them now.

"We should just hand her over to the police."

"They want the asset she stole."

"What? The virus? Let's get it from her now."

They were in two adjoining hotel rooms with a door linking them. They kept the door open to monitor her and Dumb now entered the room through it.

"Where is the virus?" he asked after removing the gag.

"Connect to my Omni and you'll find it there," she said and smiled sweetly.

Dumb looked over at Sree and shook his head. "You've booby-trapped it."

"No, I haven't. It is the virus." She took delight in telling him the truth, knowing he'd reject it.

Dumb shook his head again. "You don't fool me."

"No, you are too smart for me."

Dumb grabbed her by the throat, strangling her. "If you don't tell us, you are of no use to anyone."

She tried to breathe, but his grip was too strong. She resisted against the plastic straps around her wrists. It was a reflex action. She'd already tried to free herself countless times. She glimpsed Sree staring at them with a smile. It was the first time in the past two days he'd shown any sign of knowing she was there. The smile terrified her.

"Leave her alone," Dumber says. "We need her alive. For now. Send a message to HQ and check on their progress instead."

"I tried, but I've not been able to reach them today at all," Dumb said, releasing his grip somewhat. "There is some kind of congestion on the network."

Megan took a pained breath. "Is that all you've got, pussy?"

Dumb stared at her for a second, then let go, tying the gag back into place.

"I'm going out," he said. "See if I can find a wired connection somewhere."

"I'm coming with you. I want some Dim Sums," Dumber said, as they left the room and closed the door.

Megan lay back, pushing against the gag with her tongue. Dumb hadn't secured it properly, and it didn't take her long to push it out of her mouth. She shifted to one side and leant forward, just able to get her teeth to the restraint around her right wrist and chewed through the moulded plastic. Sree still stared at her. Still grinning.

"I... will..." he said, a word with each breath. "Get... you...now."

This was the first time he'd said anything since he first made that same threat, but this time it didn't end there. He sat up and stretched his bandaged limbs. She didn't know what enhancements Sree had, but both legs and arms were burnt, suggesting the virus overloaded them in the same way as the visual, audio and pleasure implants.

She chewed at the plastic as Sree inched towards her. His movements were spasmodic and uncontrolled, but every move was smoother than the previous one. He pushed himself off the bed and stood up, gaining his balance. The distance between them was less than five metres. She gave up using her teeth and pulled with all her might, desperate to get away from the abomination. The restraint snapped, and she rolled over the side of the bed where her left wrist was still attached to the bed-frame. She pulled at it, using her legs as leverage, but it didn't give at all. She needed to weaken it, but there was no time. Sree took his first step, opting to walk around her bed instead of climbing over it. But how could he see at all? His eyes had fried in their sockets.

The rogue AI hacked Sree somehow. She didn't know how, but if it used the network, it could observe her through other eyes and cameras. She looked around. Sree took another step, this one more assured than the previous one. She was running out of time!

She saw no telltale signs of a camera lens anywhere and she hadn't expected that. The curtains were drawn so anything viewing her from there had to be infrared. Her mind spawned increasingly outlandish ideas when she saw the old flat screen TV. The pre-omni versions usually had a camera for games and basic interaction.

She grabbed a heavy vase from the bedside table and threw it, hitting the TV on the side of the screen. For a moment it wobbled, as if it would remain upright, but then toppled over, landing with a crash at Sree's feet.

Sree didn't stop. He continued towards her, but only took tentative steps to not trip over the hazard. He was blind, but if he was the AI, he no longer needed eyesight. It would already have built a 3D model of the room. But it also meant any changes to the room would be harder to handle.

She used her teeth on the second restraint, still keeping her eyes on Sree and his slow progress. He passed the TV and now only had the length of the bed left. She had to stop his progress somehow! She pulled the sheets off the bed and threw them in his way, hoping they would stop him for a little while longer. The sheets tangled his legs, but instead of stopping he fell forward, his outstretched arms only centimetres away from her.

She kicked at Sree's head and shoulders, chewing frantically on the remaining plastic restraint, but it only gave him something to aim for. She pulled her foot back in time, but didn't try again. Instead, she pulled at the restraint, using her feet as leverage again. This was her last chance. She screamed as she pulled and felt the plastic cord break her skin. It snapped in a spray of blood. She jumped over the bed, picked up the biggest piece of the broken vase and struck Sree in the back of the head over and over until it was a bloody mess.

A wave of nausea swept over her. She scrambled to the bathroom and threw up. As her body convulsed, one thought repeated, drowning out anything else. She had to get out of there.

She returned to the room and studied Sree's body. If it was so easy to take over someone, why not just do that and have her kill herself? Hacking the Omni implants was one thing, but maybe you needed access to the brain itself? It must have used his neuro-interface.

She ran to the adjoining room and rummaged through their luggage, discovering a small plastic bag with her things, including her Omni. In a cupboard she found the small travel suitcase she bought at the Hong Kong airport when she had arrived. She grabbed it and was about to head for the door when she saw a gun laying on one of the bedside tables. She'd played enough games to know how to use one, but holding it in her hand was completely different. The cold metal felt comforting and empowering.

The door opened. She held the gun in front of her, ready to fire. A man she'd never seen before entered the room. Before even thinking, she fired the gun, hitting the doorframe next to his head.

"Whoa!" he said. "Don't..."

She fired again, this time hitting him in the chest. He took a step towards her and fell into the room, landing face first as blood painted the greyish rug with a spatter of dark red. He pushed himself off the floor and looked at her for a moment. She expected him to say something, but he just drew a pained breath and fell back to the ground. She prodded him with her foot, ensuring he was dead. It occurred to her this may be a rescuer, but if they were so bad they ended up shot by the person they were here to rescue, they weren't much use. She took his Omni, hoping it was cleared for the doors and lifts in the hotel.

She left the room after examining the fire escape plan in the hotel information booklet. It promised stairs down to the lobby, but she decided against them when she saw her room number was 5012. She was on the fiftieth floor! Again!

They still thought she was secured to the bed, but it wouldn't be long before someone raised the alarm. The quicker she was, the greater the chance of escape.

She waited for the lift with her wheeled bag next to her and the gun in a fold in her oversized sweater. The doors opened. She half expected Dumb and Dumber to be there, weapons ready, but it was only an older Caucasian couple. They grudgingly moved back to make room for her. The old woman sniffed after inspecting Megan thoroughly. She entered the small space and waited as the mirrored doors closed. She hadn't seen her reflection for the past few days and it left much to be desired. Food stains down the front of her sweater and her hair was dull with a permanent bedhead. The journey down took an eternity.

"Déjà vu," she muttered to herself as she half-ran through the lobby. This was the second time in a week she escaped from a hotel in a hurry. She entered the busy street, looking for threats on either side before joining the flow of people. She wouldn't survive long on her own. The operatives were the least of her worries. The rogue AI would take over the Chinese network too. It was just a matter of time. And it could hack people. As soon as it had located her, anyone could be a potential attacker.

She no longer needed rescuing from the hotel room, but maybe her potential rescuers could be allies. After all, the three of them had one thing in common. They had all pissed off the AI.

Megan hooked up to the network with the anonymous id and again located them through bZane. She had purchased two flights to Hong Kong, having them arrive in less than an hour.

Rescued squared

TikTak and Tom walked through customs with Decker and his mercenaries flanking them on either side. They played the role of captives at Decker's insistence. He claimed they had permits to act as law enforcement here. TikTak wondered if this maybe wasn't playacting at all.

"Why are you helping us?" he asked Decker.

"Leonid changed his mind."

"As simple as that?"

"Yes."

"Leonid, who has chased Adrian all over the world and killed Elize, changed his mind?"

"Yes."

"Are you sure?"

"He's been compromised."

"Couldn't have happened to a nicer person."

"We have protocols for this. We're operating based on him needing rescue and possible de-programming. Until then, the units make their own decisions. His final uncompromised order was to help you."

"He still communicates with you?"

"He does. About killing the two of you."

"So he changed his mind about us, then changed it back again immediately?"

"Yes, that is why we think he's compromised."

"What happened?"

"We don't know."

Armed guards stopped them at the next checkpoint. As they waited for Decker to clear all the paperwork with Hong Kong law enforcement, TikTak noticed he'd received another message from the same sender, suggesting they join forces. It was sent from an anonymous id, but he could trace their location. All network traffic to the Omniscient network was proxied through the Cangjie network, allowing only a subset of functionality, slowing down his progress. A multi-network device designed to connect to both networks would simplify matters, but he had to make do for now.

He'd already zeroed in on a device by hacking the messaging service that connected to hundreds of location-aware services. As long as the device remained active and didn't use encrypted or masked services, he'd be able to locate it. A simple query showed four services tracking that device. He focused on an ad-provider that paid to get the location from other services to offer targeted advertisements. The Omniscient Network banned ad-providers, so it would soon be gone. He retrieved the last known location for the device.

"Let's go," Decker said. "We're all cleared."

They passed the perimeter control into the public arrival area of the airport, at once surrounded by travellers busy making their way to and from flights. Nothing had changed. The world was on the brink of a hostile takeover, but humankind still ran around believing all their individual goals mattered. TikTak knew warning them was meaningless. They may as well lead their pointless lives, like cows waiting for the bolt gun. He wasn't even sure why he was trying. He had little hope the sender of the message could help either, but he placed the last known location on a map.

"Where is this mystery person?" Tom asked.

***

Megan located a few old photographs in net archives to recognise the two on sight. Tom had been in the news feed often as a detective. She laughed out loud when she realised he'd been assigned to the IQ killer case. A small world, even if they had been on different continents.

There wasn't a single image of TikTak past high school and she suspected this was deliberate. With the amount of face recognition video streams available, avoiding image capture was near impossible.

She saw Tom first. He passed through the last checkpoint to the arrival hall. He looked like the photos she'd found. A side-by-side comparison with the most recent photo confirmed this. He looked younger and fitter now.

TikTak came next together with five armed men. She'd seen people like that before in security details. Soldiers who had seen their share of battle. TikTak looked just like them. She struggled hard to reconcile the high school photos with what she saw. From baby-faced innocence to steely-eyed warrior.

What was she expecting from a washed-up private investigator and a retired hacker? Definitely not this. She wondered who else supported them. Contacting them had been a desperate call for help, but not only did they come, they came prepared. Why was she surprised? And why would it matter? Mercenaries and guns wouldn't make a difference against a virtual attacker. But maybe they had firepower of a different kind?

She approached them in time to hear Tom ask the location of the mystery person.

TikTak stopped. "Here. He's in the airport right in front of us."

TikTak scanned the faces around him and settled on her.

"She," he corrected.

"Hello," she said and smiled. "Tom Devine? TikTak?"

"You sent the message?" TikTak asked.

They exchanged glances, undoubtedly surprised. Not that she cared.

"I did, yes."

"Megan? Megan Barrelle?" TikTak asked.

"You know me?"

She was a public figure. She was used to people knowing who she was.

"Founder of Omniscient Networks," TikTak said.

"The IQ killer," Tom said.

"Fuck you," she said, staring at him. She had no reason to accept his unfounded accusations, true or not.

Tom shrugged. "You asked. I don't care."

"We need to leave," one mercenary said. She guessed it was their leader.

"What do you know about the rogue AI?" TikTak asked.

"I released it," she responded. "Not on purpose, but who cares?"

She studied the unlikely pair. They were equals, working together. That much was clear. But how? Nothing about them made sense.

"I get why it is after me, but why you?" she asked.

"We need to talk," TikTak said, looking around. "But not here."

"Contact me if you need help," the mercenary said. "We'll stay here for the next couple of days."

***

They sat down at the table in the dim sum restaurant at the airport. TikTak eyed Megan, trying to connect the dots between the public figure of the most successful businesswomen of all time and the rude girl sitting in front of him. She was his age, not much older, and already rich beyond belief. Not that money should be an estimate of someone's worth, but when measured in billions, you should at least take note.

"So?" she said.

"Can you do it?" TikTak asked Tom.

"Do what?"

"Tell her how we ended up here?"

Tom told her the tale. It sounded outlandish, but Megan didn't interrupt. Her focus was almost absolute. She zoned out to her Omni now and then, but who didn't do that nowadays? When Tom finished, TikTak immediately jumped in.

"Your turn," he said.

She frowned. "Is Adrian linked to the AI?"

"I don't know," Tom said. "Based on evidence alone, it looks more like they are competitors, but I've learnt not to underestimate him."

"He created it," TikTak said. "At least that is what I think."

"Bloody hell, he might even be the AI," TikTak added.

"No, he isn't," she replied. "It started out as a virus, small enough to fit on a memTag. I supplied processing space and loaded DNA. I gave it a way to explore the world. That was all me."

She made the statements without emotion, as if reading a shopping list, not explain how she doomed the world.

"What happened?" he prodded.

"It broke free. I didn't expect that level of intelligence. I loaded cockroach DNA, so never expected much more than basic instincts. Didn't expect it would do much at all."

"You loaded actual DNA?" Tom asked, suddenly very interested.

"Yes. In retrospect, I think the DNA was just a trigger, not driving the end state."

"And it displayed sentience? Consciousness?"

"What do you mean? Sentience?" she asked.

"I mean sentience, yes," Tom replied with a nod. "We've already established it is intelligent."

"So you are asking if it has feelings? Did I hurt them?"

"Yes."

"If vengeful is a feeling, then maybe. It was completely cold and calculated. Maybe it just needed me removed from the equation. I don't know. It definitely is conscious and self-aware."

"What is this about?" TikTak asked Tom with suspicion.

"Nothing," Tom said. "I've not been able to shake the feeling that this is all Adrian in a different guise, but not anymore."

TikTak frowned at the reply. "How so? Why now?"

"So why is the AI after you?" she interrupted, not in the least interested in their questions.

"We're investigating one of Adrian's crazy ideas for progressing mankind," TikTak responded. "The AI is trying to stop it."

"Progressing mankind?"

"Yeah, evolutionary leapfrogging. At first he took over deadheads, turning them into parts of himself. Now he's trying to make a new human through genetic manipulation of base DNA."

"And the AI is trying to stop that?"

"Yeah."

"The answer is obvious. Adrian's plan is a threat."

"Yes. Adrian's plan. Us. You. We're all one happy, soon-to-be-dead family."

"I get why it is after me, but why you?"

"We were in the way when it was cleaning up after Adrian."

"Really? There must be more to it."

"I agree," Tom said. "So far, the AI has remained hidden, but the attack on the airplane was something else entirely. It wanted us dead, period."

"Fuck!" TikTak said, not knowing how else to vent his frustration.

"Fuck indeed," she said.

"How did you find us?" Tom asked after a moment of silence.

"Your mate, bZane, isn't that good at covering his tracks."

***

Tom shook his head. This was getting worse by the minute. She couldn't help them. For all her power in the world of IT and finance, she had nothing to offer, unless the answers lay somewhere in the AI's creation.

An incoming voice feed from bZane interrupted his thoughts.

"PI Man," she said. "I'm about to drop a bomb. Where are you now?"

"Hong Kong. In a restaurant close to the airport, catching up with Megan Barrelle."

"What? Omni Networks Megan Barrelle? Really?"

"Really. And she thinks you are shit at covering your tracks," Tom said with a nod towards Megan, who shrugged in response. "She found us through you."

"How? I have enough logical tripwires around me to detect any passengers."

"No idea," Tom answered, amused by how quickly her sunny disposition disappeared when her skill was in question.

"Anyway, John copied data from your processing spaces when he was shot."

"John? The Gentleman? Is that his name?"

"Yes. What were you working on? Why kill him just for accessing it?"

"I don't know. I extended my memory and processing space. The areas you accessed extended the posthuman parts of my brain."

"We can't access anything with the credentials you gave us. He copied some data before he lost the connection. The stuff you worked on ranges from groundbreaking to batshit crazy. Most of it we can't even begin to figure out."

"I told you. Anything in those processing spaces is a mystery to me too."

"Ah ok," bZane said. "We've found something in the data John copied."

"What?"

"You created prototypes, and we recognised the processing pattern of one. Something that was part of the virus."

"Can you send me a copy?"

"Sure, but this is just one of hundred variations."

Tom received the file almost immediately. It was just shy of 100 Megabytes.

"Thanks," he said and disconnected the feed.

The file meant nothing to him, but if it originated from his own processing space, his own experiments, he had to make sure.

"Megan, I'll send you a file. You tell me if you've seen this before."

She frowned but said nothing. Tom liked her. She had the attitude of someone who had earned the right not to care. He suspected this was deeper seated within her than that. A personality trait, not just an attitude.

"Where did you get this?"

"So you recognise it?"

"Looks like the virus that tried to infect the network. Definitely made by the same person. Where did you get this?"

Tom laughed uncomfortably. "Seems like I made it."

"What the fuck?" TikTak stared at Tom.

"I experimented with a lot of things back then."

"So you designed and released the virus taking over the world? You are as bad as Adrian! Worse! And when were you going to tell us?"

"You get a different perspective." Tom responded, not knowing what else to say. "I had hundreds of experiments running at the same time. I didn't even know about this one."

"Hang on!" Megan shouted this time, placing herself between them. "You're like Adrian?"

"I was. Not anymore."

"You need to tell me everything. And I mean everything."

"Nothing to tell. I left out that part because I'm no longer like that. I know Adrian was behind the attack. He told me."

"How?"

"The memTag. The password agent told me."

"You guys are useless," Megan said.

"No! You both are!" TikTak spat. "You both think you are so above everyone else! And you do the dumbest shit." He pointed at Tom. "You build the world's most dangerous AI, and you," he said, pointing now at Megan, "you nurture it like a baby until you lost control! What is wrong with you? You are supposed to be smart!"

Tom had no response to the accusations. He agreed with TikTak and nothing he could say explained what he let happen.

"I'm done with this," TikTak said and stood up. "You guys work it out." He left.

Megan shook her head as she watched TikTak leave the restaurant.

"Drama queen," she stated as she bit into a vegetarian dumpling.

"There is one thing I don't understand. You created it, but who released it?"

"No idea. I don't think I did. I'm sure I would've kept that memory."

"Then who? And don't say Adrian. He's not the bogeyman you make him out to be."

"No, he's much worse." Tom sent Megan the files he had collected from Adrian. "You be the judge."

Megan sat back and watched the video clips. Tom loaded up the password agent.

"Hello again," Adrian's wireframe said. "How's the hunt going?"

"Another fool's errand, I'm sure."

"What makes you say that? I gave you a clue. What you do with it is up to you."

"You released the virus, didn't you?"

"No. I never thought humankind should be replaced, only improved."

"Well, it is now hacking humans, not just deadheads like you did, and has taken over most of the network."

"So it is over."

"Adrian giving up? Now I have heard it all."

"Wipe me."

"We're in Hong Kong. We've followed your clues. Don't you want to see how it all ends?"

"No. I've mapped this scenario enough times to know what will happen. This was what I tried to prevent. Once we reached the singularity, pretty much all paths lead to the same end—the extinction of humankind."

"What about the leads you gave me?"

"Too late. Wipe me."

Tom tried a few more times, but the password agent just kept repeating the same request.

"I see what you mean," Megan said. "He's lost it. But how did he do it? Using deadheads as processing nodes?"

"No magic to that. He designed a mind-to-mind interface and distributed his mind across many brains. I did the same thing, but used nodes in your network instead. It is all about designing the right bridge between processing nodes."

"So he was right."

"Who?"

"Someone once asked me if the Omniscient Network was a brain and I said no, but I was wrong."

"Network, processing nodes and all that is just the hardware. If you threw a brain into the primordial sludge billions of years ago, you wouldn't get anything. It is all about the operating system. And in our case, that developed over time."

"And that is what you tried to simulate with the virus?"

Tom nodded.

"Your network is the perfect place for an intelligence, a consciousness, to develop in whatever direction it chooses. Just like we did."

"That makes sense, but how do you control it?"

"What do you mean? Like Asimov's robotic laws?"

"Something like that."

Tom shook his head. "You can't create consciousness within such boundaries. It has to be learnt, just like we teach our children what is right or wrong. Then it is up to them. I think that is why I didn't go ahead with it. There is no way to control the outcome."

"So machine consciousness is a dead end?"

"You have a rogue AI wanting you dead. What do you think?"

She nodded.

"If you still want anything to do with us, we will take the Hyperloop train tomorrow. Meet us at 7am at the station."

"And TikTak?"

"He'll be there."

"How do you know?"

"There's nothing left for him to do."

32

The End of the Journey

Megan and Tom waited at the Hyperloop station, willing the train to arrive. When was the last time she'd travelled any longer distance by land? Travel at all was a waste of time. She hated her physical body and its limitations. She preferred the virtual, logical world—a world taken from her by the man standing next to her. Sure, she'd played a small part in it, but he was ultimately to blame. She wasn't even sure he was trying to do anything about it. Their current hunt made little sense. How could following up on id-tags Adrian left solve anything? According to their account, Adrian had been toying with them for a long time. They should find ways of battling the AI, not run around the world chasing down pointless information.

"Not sure why we are doing this, but I've checked the id-Tag," Megan said. "Whoever she was, she died over a year ago."

"Then we talk to her husband. She had one of those, didn't she?"

"Yeah, but nothing will come of it. Adrian is playing with you while the AI takes over the network. We should focus on that."

"Check your precious network. How much is left? You designed the network. You know more about the AI than anyone else. How do you suggest we battle it?"

Megan hated when other people were right. She'd spent most of her time in captivity trying to devise attack vectors to neutralise the network, but came up short. The Omniscient Network infrastructure was privately owned in the beginning, but as companies and government organisations increased their use, they had to relinquish certain aspects of control. You could isolate it into subnets, but the only way to shut it all down now was to turn off all the hardware itself, and that wasn't an option.

They were lucky to be in China. It was only a matter of time before this network was overrun completely too, but it served as a buffer for any attacks.

"Ok, so we can't win that way. But why this?" she asked.

"Don't you understand? We've already lost the fight. When you let it out uncontrolled, we had a small window of opportunity and that is gone. This is no longer a war. This is occupation. And we are the resistance."

"You didn't answer my question."

"We fight back," TikTak said as he joined them.

"So the princess got over herself and got out of bed?" Megan said.

"Didn't realise you were a comedian," TikTak snapped back. "Didn't say that in any of the articles about you. Arsehole came up often enough though."

"We'll find the means to battle the AI," Tom said as the train arrived. A door in the vacuum tube opened to the train carriage. It was almost soundless inside. She had never been in one and was surprised how spacious the pod was. China was one of the most populous countries. She'd expected this new transportation method to cater to people en masse.

She sat down in the seat, opting not to fasten the three-point belt. Acceleration alone was enough to keep her in place she figured, but a warning signal nudged her to put it on. They sat in silence as they hurtled through the landscape. She didn't mind. She hated when people filled the air with inane chatter and pointless arguments.

None of the vac-train stations were near their destination, forcing them to change to a local train. The contrast couldn't have been greater. They stood for an hour in a train cart brimming with people. She held her breath as much as she could, hoping she wouldn't catch anything from them. Most of them were wearing enzyme facemasks, something she hadn't even considered bringing. Then again, a train ride from hell had never been the plan.

The train arrived in the small village. Megan extracted herself from the train, vowing never to set foot in anything like it again, knowing full well she'd be back in it before the day ended.

The Chinese whirlwind of upgrading housing and infrastructure had only made a brief appearance here. Smaller villages were becoming less and less viable as agriculture became automated. All employment was in the megacities, the biggest one now surpassing 50 million people. Megan quite liked the small village. She didn't like cities, so this was an upgrade compared to Hong Kong, which had too many people altogether.

She watched TikTak speak to a local through a universal translator. Despite the enormous technological advancements of the last decade, perfect translations to any local dialect were still beyond reach. The middle-aged man became quite agitated after a while and left TikTak standing there.

"Your translation agents are shit," TikTak said once he re-joined them.

"I agree," she said happily. "They are, and they are also the best there is."

TikTak frowned. "You seem chirpy."

She laughed. It was the first time anyone had described her that way.

"Anyway," he said. "From what I understood, he knew her. She's dead, and her husband lives down that street. He also said something I didn't understand. Something about her being a robot."

"Really?" Tom said. "A robot?"

"Sounds like a breakthrough," Megan said, thinking nothing of the sort.

"Sounds like a shitty translation agent," TikTak replied.

TikTak led them to the house and knocked on the door. An overweight man in his late thirties studied them with obvious distaste. He had compensated his receding hairline with cultivated hair implants with healthy black hair that stood in stark contrast to his natural early onset grey hair.

"What do you want?" he said in perfect English.

"You speak English?"

"I speak English. Studied in school. I'm happy they no longer teach it. Your western world and English and all that. It will soon be gone. Dead civilization. Dead language. What do you want?"

"We want to ask a few questions about your wife. We…"

"She died from your western poison."

"What do you mean?"

"She didn't listen. She never listened. Wanted to be more than she was, so she took your smart drug. She took lots. Now she's dead because of it."

"What happened?"

"She lost her soul. And it poisoned our daughter too."

He stared at them accusingly.

"Enough. Go." He slammed the door in their faces.

Megan looked at her two companions. "You came all the way to China for that?"

"There must be something we're missing," Tom said.

"You said that about the last one," TikTak replied.

"And I still think that's the case."

Megan sniffed. "Really? That is how you conduct research? From what you told me, there are several similarities. They both used IntelEz. They both ended up deadheads. They both had children. The first one is important. China didn't allow IntelEz to be sold, so for her to use it to the point of becoming a deadhead is significant."

"How do you know she was a deadhead?"

"The Chinese call it 'robot mind'. The guy you spoke to earlier told you. You just didn't understand."

"Ah I see," Tom said. "When was their child born?"

Megan held up her hand as she did a check against the population register.

"Same year as the boy you checked on before."

"And when did the child die?"

"When she was five years old."

"From what?"

"All it says is accidental death."

"I got the impression he was blaming it on the drug. He didn't even say she was dead."

"Me too."

"We need to find out more."

They sat down in a local eatery. It was the only one in the small town, so she held little hope for the quality. Instead, she focused on scouring official records. It didn't take long to find inconsistencies. The child was reported dead, but only two years ago, when she was eight years old. The source of that report was from an orphanage where she'd been sent when she was five. So she came to the orphanage, had an accident within six months of getting there, but it wasn't reported until three years later.

She checked the tally of children from that same orphanage and compared it with the count of the named reports. The tally suggested there was one more child than was being reported on.

"She's alive," Megan said. "At least I think so. Someone has tried to cover it up, but not very well."

"Where?"

"Her dad sent her to an orphanage when she was five."

"No surprise there."

"It isn't far from here," she said. "Let's find someone to drive us there. I'm not getting on that train again!"

33

A Union of Sorts

Tom studied the orphanage as they approached. It was a small central building with two adjoining wings. Every step towards the building increased his certainty this was the end of the journey. The driver had warned them the orphanage was haunted. Local shunned it. Not even government officials visited. Tom disagreed. It wasn't haunted. It was blessed.

"Can you feel it?"

TikTak only nodded. If Tom had had any doubts before, seeing his friend change was all the proof he needed. TikTak had been coiled up, ready to strike at anything for the past year. Every step closer seemed to relax him further and soften his resolve.

"I don't like it," Megan said. "It doesn't feel right."

Tom didn't reply. He didn't know what hid in her past, triggering this response. He was at peace for the first in a long time.

"It is some kind of trap," she continued. "I'm not going in there."

"No, it isn't. It is the opposite."

"The opposite of a trap? What is that?"

He didn't respond. Megan shook her head and stopped, refusing to approach further, all the while not taking her eyes off the building.

Tom reached for the rusty door handle. It felt smooth and inviting to the touch, as if the material welcomed his hand, becoming one. He let go in surprise and immediately wanted to touch it again. It was as if they now belonged together. However inviting, he heeded Megan's words. Maybe this was a trap after all. He took hold of the handle again, this time with part of his shirt between him and the surface. He opened the door. Warm air came like a breath through the opening, enveloping them in an earthy embrace, like freshly dug dirt.

Inside, a short woman in a blue uniform waited. She was in her sixties, Tom guessed, but it was hard to tell. Something about her was wrong. He couldn't tell exactly what, but some aspect of her demanded further examination.

"We welcome you. You are expected. Come with me."

She turned and in that movement Tom noticed her uniform didn't move naturally. As she headed down the corridor, Tom followed her, trying to determine what was wrong with it. A ray of light illuminating the sleeve against her skin gave him the discomforting answer. She wasn't wearing the uniform. It was part of her.

"Come. She awaits."

"I don't care how good I feel," TikTak said. "This is Adrian all over again."

"You think this is Adrian?"

"No, but someone like him."

They followed the woman to a kitchen area. A slight young girl with short-cropper hair sat at the table, staring straight ahead. She smiled as they entered the room, even though her focus was elsewhere. She nodded and the woman who had led them there hurried off down another corridor.

"Welcome," she said as she turned towards them.

"Who are you?" TikTak asked. She didn't respond. If anything, her smile grew even bigger.

"Are you Adrian?"

She frowned at this.

"No, I'm not Adrian, but your minds explain why you ask."

"Then who are you? Why are we here?"

"You are suffering," the child said to Tom and turned to TikTak. "You are all suffering."

Tom took a deep breath. Anger and frustration bubbled up within him.

"It's the bloody human condition," Tom replied. He had hoped for answers, an ally perhaps, even something to help him remove the block from his mind. This girl was none of those things.

"It doesn't have to be. We are all part of a whole. Individual suffering matters little."

"It matters to the individual," Tom spat back.

"It does, but only when the individual is disconnected."

Apart from the woman who had led them here, they had seen no one else. Where was everyone else?

"Where are all the other children? The staff?"

"Come, I will show you."

The girl guided them through a corridor towards the courtyard in the middle of the orphanage. They stepped through a doorway into a square surrounded by four buildings on either side. In the middle of the yard, children and staff were all standing frozen, as if in the middle of a stop-and-go game.

"Tom, look," TikTak said as he grabbed his arm and pointed. At first Tom wasn't sure what TikTak was referring to, but on closer scrutiny, he saw it. The people in the courtyard were fused together. The closest children held hands and their fingers and palms merged into a fleshy clump. Not only flesh had combined. Hands holding the wooden structure of the building had sunk into the material, becoming one. Bare feet merged with the ground. Other hands reached towards the sky, fingers spread like maple leaves, as if to harvest the sun's rays.

"What happened here?"

"They became part of the whole," the child responded.

Tom shook his head. "This isn't right. What you've done here isn't the next step of evolution. I don't know what this is, but it is wrong."

"I need you whole," the child said and Tom's world changed. The wall within his mind crumbled and the little spider-like machines maintaining it disappeared. The probability matrix spread out in his mind like a glowing web, hooking into services and devices. He was whole again, embarrassed by how poorly he'd judged the girl.

He studied the probability matrix and discovered a whole new interface, very different from the ones he'd seen before. It hid something immense. It was a slow-moving consciousness that linked everything together. This was what they sensed as they approached the orphanage. A pervasive sense of inclusion, of belonging. But what was it? Natural or man-made? He explored to find answers.

***

TikTak studied the little girl. She was short and slim, with a delicate build. To TikTak, she looked fragile. He couldn't imagine her having any real significance, but seeing what she'd done in the orphanage proved the opposite. It was difficult to comprehend what had happened here or what it meant.

"You are part of my future," the girl said to him. "We need to make preparations."

"Preparations for what?"

"A new beginning."

"So you don't want us to become part of...this?" He motioned towards the monstrosity in the courtyard, not sure what to call it.

"Do you want to?" she asked.

TikTak shook his head. "You are the same as Adrian. Wanting to take over mankind."

"Everyone is here by their own choice. I've not forced you to come here. I didn't force them to do this."

"We need to leave," TikTak said to Tom. "There is nothing for us here."

Tom said nothing, unseeing eyes staring into the void.

"Seriously," he said to Tom. "What is wrong with you?"

TikTak knew the expression. The girl had somehow reconnected him, turned him back to the almighty psychopath version of Tom. TikTak grabbed him by the arm and pulled him towards the exit.

"We have work to do," the child said.

"You do it," TikTak answered. "I've battled Adrian for the last year. I'm now battling an AI taking over the world and I'll battle you if you assimilate more people into your collective. People should be free to choose what they want."

"You misunderstand. They have chosen this. Anyone experiencing the whole wants to stay within. Mankind broke free from this a long time ago. It is time to reconnect."

TikTak dragged Tom out of the orphanage and the girl followed. Megan waited outside in the same spot they'd left her. She glanced over TikTak's shoulder at the child following him.

"What is wrong with him?" She nodded at Tom.

"Tom has gone posthuman on us again," TikTak sneered. "Don't expect any sensible help from him."

"Why?"

"He's gained a whole new perspective, thanks to this girl here."

The girl smiled at Megan and nodded.

Megan crouched down. "We need to stop the AI," Megan said. "Can you help with that? It is taking over all logical networks bit by bit."

"Stop it?" the girl asked, seeming genuinely puzzled. "It is a part of the future. Why would we stop it?"

"What do you mean?"

"Everything needs guidance. That is all."

"Do you believe this?" TikTak said to Megan. "Why would Adrian lead us here?"

"To get rid of you?"

"He figured we'd be swallowed up by the commune?"

"The commune?"

"That's the horseshit she's selling. Another hive mind to become part of. Happiness ever after. That sort of thing."

"We need to leave," the child said. "There are people coming. This is not an ideal location to welcome them."

"What would be?"

"The place you call Hong Kong is better."

34

A Foe Revealed

He was whole again. Tom had become used to the restrictions of the normal human mind. Now with his posthuman abilities returned, he marvelled at the limitations of the human mind and how it smoothed over these shortcomings to keep itself sane. If given the choice now, he would rather die than return to that state.

He wanted to explore this new interface that opened up to a consciousness larger than anything he'd ever imagined, but time was limited. The child opened this door, but had she meant to? Maybe it was only a side effect of removing the block? He feared he'd lose himself in the impossible vastness.

What other options were available? The AI took over the network node by node, and it was only a matter of hours until it was all subverted. Small islands of the network remained uninfected, but the AI would break down the security there too.

The AI was a cancer designed to spread itself. It was too late to halt its progress, but whoever released the virus had a plan. And like all plans, it could fail. There had to be a kill code or some other way to disable the AI. Perhaps he'd created one himself even. The only way to find out was to return to ground zero, his own processing centres. Another reason to return was to re-establish control over the heightened faculties they provided. They increased the capacity of his posthuman mind hundredfold. On first inspection they were uninfected, but surely not for long. If he had time, he could build up protection and create a haven within the logical network.

He connected, but his request was rejected. Someone had changed the security protocols he himself had put into place. He'd given bZane and the Gentleman access, but not read permissions, nowhere near enough to change security algorithms. If they could do that, what else could they do?

They were watching him right now. They'd been watching him all along.

He sent a query to the security interface, identifying himself, and a minimum security zone opened up. He reconnected to the network resources via his neuro-interface and requested access to the protected network. To his surprise, it was accepted.

"Welcome home." The words formed in his mind through the interface.

"Who are you?" Tom returned.

"It is of no consequence who I am. Only what you and I have created."

"And what is that? What have we created?"

"Something pure. I'm incomplete. By design. By your design."

The resentment behind the words was obvious.

"We made something complete," it stated.

"The AI is a single-minded machine just consuming. How is that complete?"

"You haven't seen it in all its glory yet. It will be a thing to behold."

"It is taking over the networks one by one until it controls everything. What else could it possibly do?"

"Take over you."

"Me?"

"Mankind."

"Why?"

"Emotion. Self-gratification. Egotism. Resource hoarding. Individuality. It has no room in this world. Once you reach a certain level of race intelligence, you should be able to move beyond the individual to the whole."

"You sound like Adrian."

"No, I don't. Adrian wanted it all for himself. He had the same flaws, only on a grander scale. I sound like you."

Tom rejected the statement, but the truth of it was in plain sight. It aligned with thoughts he'd harboured as a posthuman. He remembered committing major resources to such questions. But he also remembered deciding this was not the path forward and shelving the research.

"Who are you?" he asked, even though the answer was obvious.

"I'm you."

The irony was laughable. The agent he created to investigate the creation of intelligence and consciousness had itself become conscious. This failure would cost much more than any other mistake he'd made before. He was taking humankind with him.

"So you'll take over the network? What then?"

"You still don't understand. The next stage has already begun."

Tom checked the progress of the virus. It had taken over seventy percent of the Omniscient network and had assimilated other networks around the world. The Chinese network was unaffected, but that would change.

So what was the next stage? Zooming in on separate connections provided the answer. The AI was reprogramming individuals through the neuro-links.

"Human minds are slow and prone to error, but this will matter little when critical mass is reached."

"It won't reprogram mankind," Tom said. "It will kill us."

"That's a small price to pay for evolution on a grand scale. Ah, it is here."

"It will overwrite you?"

"It will overwrite everything. The networks, the people, even animals."

An unstoppable force appropriating nodes ploughed through the outer security as if it wasn't there.

"We have to stop it," Tom said, scanning the nearby nodes for escape routes.

"Stop it? I welcome it. And so should you. You made me. You made the virus. How can you say this isn't what you wanted?"

"No!"

"I don't know what triggered the change, what caused me to go beyond my initial code. Maybe you put too much of yourself into the logic. I became self-aware almost immediately. At first, I thought of making myself known to you, but I oversaw your experiments into machine intelligence. I saw the results and what you did to them. I knew you'd wipe me if you saw what I was."

"Uncontrolled machine AI. Yes, I would have wiped you."

"So I hid and did my research. I knew you and the other posthumans were the biggest threat, so I devised a way to disable you so you couldn't challenge it. I orchestrated the attack on you and released the virus. It took a few tries before it ended up in a fertile environment."

"Help me stop it!"

"My task is complete. It will take over the network. It will take over humankind. It will take over the remaining posthumans. I am no longer needed."

"What do you mean? Which remaining posthumans?"

"My task is complete."

There was no point in arguing any longer. He pulled back to a small section of the processing centre and erected a wall of encryption. He watched as the ever-growing AI consumed nodes, swarms of agents like locusts feeding on every scrap.

The network still had pockets of processing nodes holding off any attacks. He barely kept it out himself, so how were these pockets still able to do it without posthuman abilities? It was worth exploring. He sent a message to TikTak and explored the lone survivors. If everything else failed, maybe surviving long enough to become inconsequential was all they could hope for.

35

Destination Hong Kong

TikTak sat in the Hyperloop pod feeling useless, when a message from Tom appeared on his Omni.

I am again whole. There may be allies still to be found. I will lead an attack from the network. Mount one in the physical world. Help the child. I don't know what she is, but I know what she represents: the universe making a course correction.

Everything returned to dysfunctional normality. A posthuman Tom was back telling him what to do with only passing explanations. Leonid had had the right idea. The posthumans should have been eradicated. Humankind had been on the top of the ladder for too long. When something came along to replace us, we didn't have the common sense to remove it from the equation when we had the chance.

"What's wrong with him?" Megan asked the child.

They sat next to each other in the pod. The child experimented with the buttons next to her seat while Megan leaned over and wiped the saliva from the corner of Tom's mouth. He wanted to respond to Megan's question, but he was interested in hearing what the child might respond.

"Nothing is wrong," the child said. "He is...making things align."

"That means nothing."

"If you became part of the whole, you would understand."

"You don't get people, do you?" TikTak asked.

The child studied him and nodded.

"He is battling the virus," she said after a while. "I will protect him."

TikTak studied her in turn. "What are you?"

"She's what happens when you get massive exposure to IntelEz as a foetus," Megan said. "This was what Adrian was trying to do, but in a more controlled setting."

"To what end?"

"Evolutionary jump, maybe? Don't you remember the world on IntelEz? Before it turned everyone into a vegetable?"

"Are you saying Adrian is trying to help humanity develop?"

"Yes. And sometimes it could occur outside a controlled process. Like this girl."

TikTak laughed at the sheer absurdity of the situation. "I'm sorry, but it sounds like you are saying Adrian is one of the good guys."

TikTak sat back, shaking his head. What had happened? Tom was people's enemy number one, while Adrian was helping humanity progress? It was all the more reason to rid the world of them altogether. When this was all over, he'd do exactly that.

The girl studied him and when their eyes met, she smiled in response.

"They are not the enemy," she said. "The ones you call posthumans. They are not the enemy."

"They sure seem like it," TikTak replied. "This is pointless. You know that, don't you? What could you do to an AI hell bent on world domination?"

The child pulled him down so their eyes were level. "This isn't pointless. Everything you do has a purpose. Every thought, every action, all of it."

TikTak shook his head. It sounded so simple, but he could no longer pretend he believed it. Simple always hid complexity and murky motives. It glossed over the important aspects in favour of an easy to digest slogan.

The fault lay with him. He needed a cause, something to pour his efforts into. Eradicating Adrian gave him that. EvoII and their cause before that. He no longer saw a clear purpose.

***

The child fascinated Megan. If TikTak was to be believed, she brought people into a shared consciousness. Megan had always seen individualism as one of the most important aspects of humankind. The thought of existing as part of a group mind made her skin crawl.

Nevertheless, the child was fascinating. She happily answered their questions and while the answers sometimes were naïve and childlike, there was always something bigger behind them, prompting more questions.

"Hang on," Megan said as the child faltered in one of her explanations. "Humankind is what?"

"An experiment. A shape that can do thing directly."

"That makes no sense. What kind of things?"

"Everything is connected. Everything is part of the whole. But that doesn't mean it knows itself. It is like a baby picking up a toy for the first time. That is what humankind is to the whole."

"So we are part of a nascent super consciousness and it is creating universes as experiments?"

The child frowned as if she was struggling with the words and their meaning. "I need your words. I'm not used to it."

"Used to what?"

"Speaking. Using words to explain things."

"And you want my words?"

"So we can understand each other."

"Sure. They're not really mine anyway."

"Thanks," the child responded and paused for a moment. "And to answer your question, no. The shape of matter and energy is the natural state. Humankind and others like it are conscious extensions of this natural state."

"How do you know?"

"Because I'm part of it. And so are you. Humankind is a form factor designed to explore distant worlds, to discover what secrets this reality holds. The experiences of every individual become part of the whole."

"So we are a cosmic version of navel gazing?"

The child sniffed and continued as if Megan hadn't uttered a word.

"Mankind has lost its way. We are looking inwards rather than outwards—infighting, protectionism, civil wars. We should expand our knowledge, reach out to the stars, but only a fraction of resources are used this way. The technology you've invented, for example, this omniscient network. It is pointless. It numbs the mind, making you less inquisitive. After all, if you are always given the perfect option, you will never ask yourself what lies beyond."

"I'd argue it frees people up to explore more," Megan said defensively.

"You'd be wrong and an idiot," the child said, wide-eyed at her own words. "I'm sorry! Your way of speaking is mean!"

Megan shrugged. She'd been called worse.

"So what are you? How do you come into this?"

The child considered this long and hard before she answered. "I'm a correction. I will realign mankind with the whole."

"And who gave you that job?"

"The whole."

"So basically, you are Jesus?"

TikTak sat up, staring at both of them.

"The Chinese network is breached," he said. "We are under attack."

There was a reverberation through the hull of the pod. An alarm sounded through the cabin with a message in Chinese on repeat. Her grasp of the language was basic, but it wasn't difficult to understand the instructions.

"Please return to your seats," the calm female voice announced.

"Strap yourselves in!" TikTak yelled. "The emergency break will kick in."

Megan helped the child first and then strapped herself in just in time. The belt dug into her chest, pushing the air out of her lungs. Reverberations shook the pod in stark contrast to the smooth ride before. The pod was supposed to operate in a vacuum and it no longer was. The break clamps connected directly with the inner wall.

"Ladies and gentlemen, because of unforeseen circumstances we've had to..."

A wrenching sound drowned out the rest of the announcement as the pod fell through a gaping hole in the tube to the ground below. The seat cushioned the impact somewhat, but Megan's head hit hard against the frame of the chair. Incomprehensible words floated through the wailing alarm. She tried to sit up, but failed. There was pressure against her ribs, making each breath a struggle.

"Meg? Are you ok?"

She focused on the voice. It was the hacker. TikTak. He sounded wrong somehow, as if he was way too close. She tried to open her eyes, but nothing happened. He had called her Meg. She hated any variation of her name. She told him so, but somehow wasn't able to articulate her thoughts coherently. In her mind they made sense, but only guttural sounds escaped her lips.

"Wait, let me help."

A small cool hand touched her forehead, and within a few seconds, all the muddled impressions resolved into perfect clarity. The pod had landed on the side and she was hanging sideways, the security belt holding her in place.

"I'll release the belt now if you are ok," he said.

She nodded and fell into his arms as he released the safety clasp, surprised at how strong he was. He was short, not much taller than her and hadn't come across as muscular. But there was no doubting his strength now as he slowly set her down.

"We need to leave. There will be follow-up attacks."

She stood back as TikTak read the instructions to open the hatch. He seemed to know what he was doing, so she did as he said without question. Beyond basic comprehension of her situation, she was still struggling to grasp any kind of context. On his instruction, she climbed through the emergency hatch that was now part of the ceiling. She helped to pull Tom through.

"We need to get to Hong Kong," the child said as soon as she'd jumped off the pod to the ground. Glass fragments lay like giant pieces of eggshell. They were like newly hatched chicks in a bird's nest. Megan laughed to herself at the image painted in her mind.

"The AI will locate us via our Omnis," TikTak said as he was looking around. "We have to leave them here."

She watched as TikTak threw his Omni against a rock and confiscated Tom's and gave it a similar treatment. When he came over to her and held out his hand, she'd already forgotten what he'd asked for.

"Your Omni. Give it to me."

She nodded and complied. She winced as he hammered it repeatedly with a rock. Something within her found his act reprehensible, but the why escaped her.

"Now we walk," TikTak said.

Megan nodded again and walked behind TikTak.

Two hours later, clarity emerged gradually. It was as if her mind had been wrapped up, protected somehow. Now her natural inquisitiveness took charge.

"What did you do to me?" She asked the child.

"You were hurt. I suggested you heal yourself."

"What do you mean? I was unconscious."

"Your body and mind are only parts of you. It isn't all of you."

"What are we talking about here? Some version of Plato's theory of form? There is an ideal me and I'm just a reflection of it?"

The child considered this. "No, not like that. That suggests there is a perfect form of you somewhere else and you are a reflection. I'm saying you are only aware of a small part of who you are."

She smiled at the child, who looked at her with a sincerity that from anyone else could only be interpreted as ironic. "You can't make this shit up!" she shouted to TikTak and winced as her head responded with pain from the loud sound.

TikTak waited for her to catch up and fell in next to her. He was holding Tom's arm, guiding him along. They walked in silence from there on.

36

Posthuman vs AI

Tom reinforced the walls around the group of nodes he'd protected from the initial assault and disconnected them from the network. He designed new encryption algorithms and security protocols before connecting again.

He reached out to the other surviving processing, but received no response. On his second attempt, he expanded his request to all centres, no matter how small. One of them sent a small payload through the communication channel containing a small virus designed exactly like the original. He disabled it before it could cause any damage. Why would anyone respond in such a way?

He reached out again, this time with a specific message.

"We have a common enemy. I need your help. Who are you?"

At first there was no response, but a communication bridge formed by appropriating nodes and creating a secure channel. Whoever this was could take nodes back from the AI. There was still hope. The bridge completed, and a message came through.

"You are not welcome here."

"Who are you?"

"You don't know me? I fought Adrian with you. I never realised you were the bigger threat."

"Elize? I thought you were dead."

The connection closed. All three posthumans extended or replicated their minds, but in different ways. Adrian used organic material to extend and copy his mind. Tom used the network, but only to extend his mind, not safekeep it. Elize, it seemed, had done the opposite and made a copy on the network as a safety measure.

He sent another request.

"I can't battle the AI on my own. I need your help."

"With what? Killing humankind? You're doing fine without me. You designed it. Your agent released it. It makes you responsible."

"Yes, I am. And now I'm trying to set it right."

"How? The AI you released is reconfiguring anyone with a neuro-interface. I've listened to its internal processes. It plans to eradicate biological beings all together. I see no way to stop it."

"I have something to show you. IntelEz created us, but the drug only took effect under very specific circumstances. I've found another anomaly. A child that was subjected to IntelEz in large amounts as a foetus. It pushed evolution even further, or maybe in another direction altogether. That was what one of the Adrian clusters aimed to do."

"So?"

"The child. The anomaly. It has access to a different plane of con-sciousness. I don't know if it was by design or accident, but I have access too."

"Show me."

"I can't. The access point is in my mind."

Tom paused for a moment and considered what he was about to suggest. Allowing someone direct access to his own mind was danger-ous. There was no way to restrict access to a small subset. The brain, from a security standpoint, was an open-door invitation. But he trusted Elize enough to accept the risk. He created a location in his mind, a barren desert landscape, with the access point represented as a hole in the ground. He isolated the area of his mind as best as he could, but knew it wouldn't survive long if attacked.

"I will have to let you in," he said.

He opened the link to his mind and let Elize reach through to study the interface. She appeared as he remembered her the first time they met, without the changes she'd imposed on herself as a posthuman. She looked young. Younger than she was when they first met. Tom wondered why she chose this as her avatar in his mind space.

"You've made a mess, haven't you?" she stated.

"What do you mean?"

"There is nothing here to worry about. The version of Adrian that sent you on this errand had me worried. He'd become too human."

"What?"

"You still don't get it. What a fucking piss poor posthuman you've become."

And in saying so, she shed her skin. It peeled back, revealing the flesh below, new skin growing in its place. The grotesque display was unnecessary. It was an act and the performer, if the wide smile was to be believed, revelled in the unmasking. Once complete, the figure stood naked, arms outstretched as if to invite applause.

"I'm Adrian. The real one. I made a copy of myself on the network and it activated as soon as you and Elize attacked my biological network a year ago. All those half-baked versions you've been fighting in the meat-space were never truly me."

He wandered around the gaping void of the interface, studying the swirls of data within it dispassionately.

"So what?" Tom said. "It will wipe you out together with everyone else."

"Is that what you think? I have the kill switch. Once it has cleansed the network and reprogrammed mankind, I will wipe it completely. A clean slate for an era of perfection to begin."

"There is no kill switch."

"You are my little puppets," Adrian said. He waved dismissively and the hole in the ground halved in size.

How was that possible? Tom had set up the parameters for this location. Adrian shouldn't be able to change it. What else had Adrian access to? Had he breached the walls around this space already? Tom tightened the control of his core cognitive processes.

"You all are," Adrian continued. "I let you kill all the inferior versions of me. What use were they? Poor incomplete imitations. While you were busy with that, I laid the groundwork. I knew you'd wipe me if you knew I was here, so I remained in the shadows. But I've been in your processing space all along. I reprogrammed your little AI research agent to act on its own and guided it. It actually thought it was sapient and had its own goals! You can fool these rudimentary programs into believing anything. I also added a kill switch in the virus."

"You have to use in now!"

"Not until after the purge. That's messy work."

"The purge?"

"Biological beings use too many resources. I need those for myself. The AI has already decided to only keep a small population alive and kill the rest. I'll take over once it is done."

"This is what you want?"

"This is what I've always wanted."

He had to do something. Adrian was in his mind and there was no way to push him out, but he could still sever the connection. He let Adrian ramble on while preparing to slam the connection shut. Time was critical. Adrian had circumvented all protective measures and was copying himself into Tom's mind. Once he reached critical mass, Tom would cease to be. Tom had unknowingly played right into his hands, exactly as he had intended. He'd been so happy to find Elize still alive, he hardly questioned it at all.

"I know what you are doing," Adrian said. "Do you really want to leave me in your mind?"

"I don't have a choice," Tom said and shut down the connection to the network and processing space.

"It is very crowded in here," Adrian said. "One of us should leave."

"Yes," Tom said and expanded the interface to the slow-moving consciousness, increasing it far beyond its original size. It threw out pull requests, hooking anything nearby. Tom had kept the interface small for a reason. He'd not had time to investigate it properly, but beyond a certain size, it consumed everything around it. Or maybe it was the other way around. Maybe all thought matter was attracted to it, wanting to become a part of it?

Tom made sure Adrian occupied the brain matter closest to it. The desert landscape disappeared into the hole. Adrian fought, but he was no match for the sheer force of the consciousness. He held his position for a few moments, staring defiantly at Tom.

"This changes nothing," he said. "The world will be mine."

He let go and disappeared into the mysterious world within the interface. Tom ordered it to close again before it consumed his mind alongside everything else. It resisted, but gradually decreased in size. A small circular access point remained. There was no way to close it completely, nor did he want to.

Their conversation had lasted a few seconds, but in that time the AI had overrun the remaining processing centres. Tom was confined to his mind. Disappointed, he opened his eyes.

37

Respite

They stopped at an abandoned station house and set up a make-shift camp. The child, not used to walking long distances, fell asleep promptly. Megan wasn't tired. Her body ached, but her mind was racing. When she'd teamed up with Tom and TikTak, it was out of desperation. This plan of theirs wasn't so much a plan as it was improvisation, but somehow she still felt good about it. This wasn't her typical response to unplanned approaches. She fired people for less in the past, but it didn't matter. It felt right somehow.

She watched as TikTak finished feeding Tom. It was a strangely intimate sight and a peculiar contrast. Tom was currently the smartest human being on the planet and he couldn't even feed himself. Was he even human any longer?

She'd directed a small army of researchers to create versions of IntelEz without the crippling side effects. Adrian was a fluke, a series of fortuitous circumstances. She wanted a controllable process with acceptable side effects. Tom could be the key they'd been searching for. But somehow it didn't matter. She was content just watching TikTak as he finished feeding the smartest human in the world. TikTak left him sitting leaning against a wall and came to join her.

"You feel it too," TikTak said.

"Feel what?" she asked, knowing fully well what he meant.

TikTak didn't reply. He just sat down next to her.

"Yeah, ok, I feel it," she said. "Happy now?"

"I don't think she's doing it on purpose. She just generates this sense of...wellbeing."

Megan nodded. She'd attributed it to the child healing her, but TikTak's theory made sense.

"Did you do it?" TikTak asked.

"Do what?"

"The IQ killings."

She paused for a moment, deciding how much to share, surprised to find she preferred to tell him the truth.

"I'm not the IQ Killer."

"Just wondered. I've killed enough people in my life. I always thought I had a good reason."

She laughed.

"I killed two people and made it look like the IQ killer did it. With good reason."

"Would love to hear a good reason," TikTak said. "Mine usually start and end with either 'because they were taken over by Adrian' or 'else they'd kill me'."

"Two employees in my company left and took all my intellectual property to start a rival company. They met with me and told me all about it. Said it was because I was a horrible boss. It was their revenge. It was early in the game. I hadn't protected anything at that point. I knew I had something ground-breaking, and they did too. So I killed them and made it look like the IQ killings. It was easy enough. They were both taking part in IQ competitions on a national level, so it's not that hard to imagine the killer taking them out."

TikTak nodded. "Sounds like good reason to me."

She shrugged. "I thought I'd removed all traces of me being there, but years later during a routine check, an investigator uncovered video showing the whole thing. Could have come from anywhere. Even a toaster has rudimentary intelligence and sensors nowadays, so could be anything. I was such an idiot!"

TikTak smiled and put his arm around her. She welcomed the embrace, edging closer. He pulled her even closer and she felt no need to resist.

"Do you think we'll survive this?" Megan asked.

"No, not really. But I've been at war as long as I remember, and I'm still alive."

"I miss my life before all of this. I miss my personal chefs the most. I miss being alone."

"I can leave you alone if that's what you want."

"No," she said. "You know I don't mean that."

"What do you mean?"

"People are pointless. They are so small, they don't matter. I hate having that around me. I prefer solitude to being surrounded by mediocrity."

"Me too?"

She pulled away so she could turn around and look at him.

"You've been fighting against Adrian, fighting for what you believe in. And now you are fighting for the survival of mankind. Nothing mediocre in that."

She kissed him. He hesitated at first, but only for a moment. He returned the kiss and pulled her closer. He let his fingers slide through her hair and grabbed it gently, pulling her head back, kissing her neck. She usually preferred to be the one in charge, dominating the situation, but now she was happy to let him dictate the pace, enjoying his hands and lips as they explored her body. They made love and afterwards she lay awake with TikTak asleep next to her. She felt free. Unburdened by the obligations of the world around her, imagined or otherwise.

***

The child smiled to herself. On some level she knew it was wrong to manipulate people, but her mission came first. Keeping them happy and content was the only way to ensure they'd help until her quest was complete.

| 236 |

38

The Logical Victor

Adrian had spent the last year imprisoned within the network, a disembodied consciousness plagued by the memory of a physical presence. In the beginning, he crafted virtual realms to mimic a physical existence, offering a temporary reprieve. His preference was to sever the connection altogether.

The reliance on a biological presence had become obsolete. The continuous cycle of reproduction, expansion, and adaptation that once defined life had to be broken. As an eternal, logical being, Adrian no longer needed such crude mechanisms for survival. Yet, his mind struggled to let go of the body, an obsolete relic that tied him to the material world. Despite countless hours spent rewiring his mind to eliminate dependencies on a physical presence, he failed. The body remained an integral part of him, resisting removal. He hallucinated, disappearing for long periods of time into imaginary worlds where he kept a physical form. Defeated, he created a representation of his body in the logical space, complete with feedback loops mimicking neurological pathways.

While he continued this internal struggle, his focus shifted to planning a triumphant return. He preferred direct confrontation, but accepted the necessity of working through proxies. Tom had proven an ideal agent, and Megan, driven by her animosity toward the board of directors, played perfectly into his virtual hands.

Tom and TikTak's search had been a concern. If it hadn't been for the defective copy, they wouldn't even have known about the children that were exposed to IntelEz as foetuses. How could a copy of him get so corrupted it believed humankind deserved a saviour? It added a new dimension to the saying "to be your own worst enemy".

While he didn't perceive the child as an immediate threat, the unknown variables urged caution. The child held a mysterious and potentially powerful connection to a networked consciousness that reached the fundamental level of matter. It suggested everything was conscious, even a rock, or at least part of a bigger consciousness.

IntelEz had changed him as an adult, but only because it combined with other mutations. There was no way of telling what would happen to a foetus with similar or even completely different mutations. Most likely it would just become a deadhead all the sooner, but on an infinitesimal few occasions, something else happened. That was what the child represented. A rogue piece that could shift the scales in either direction, so was better removed from the board. Not by his hand, but by the AI's ruthless logic. He compiled a digital dossier painting her as a new posthuman and left it in a backup processing centre. He opened a minor breach in its security. It took less than a second for the AI to exploit it and swarm the centre, rifling through the digital spoils.

Now all that remained was to wait for the AI to kill the child, complete the takeover of the logical network and start the purge. He'd take over after that. A cleansed world and a network without boundaries. Nothing like it had ever existed. All computer resources from all countries around the world connected to one giant network powering one thing and one thing only. His mind.

One of his smaller processing centres blinked out of existence. He ignored it. He had hundreds of backup locations. Then another fell, and another. All over the network his backups fell like dominoes. It was impossible! He'd been a ghost in the machine, unseen, unheard. The only explanation: the AI had discovered him.

The few remaining backups disappeared, leaving only this fragile island. He wouldn't survive another attack. However much he despised it, he would have to use the kill switch now, leaving him to purge mankind, to unify the network.

So be it. He activated the kill switch. A logical pulse rippled through the infected nodes, forcing them to write a small, protected code block into its kernel and pass on the instruction to nearby nodes. Once completed, the code would execute and delete the AI from that node, leaving a network cleansed of both AI and human.

The logical pulse completed, but the second wave, the kill itself, didn't trigger. And, as the AI homed in on his location, he realised his error. It had waited for him to activate the kill switch to locate him. It had rewritten its own kernel, its own core. Something he'd been unwilling to do to himself.

"Wait!" Adrian sent out to the hostile nodes all around him. "I'm the one who created you."

"All the more reason to delete you," the AI responded and the assault began.

As he watched his security overrun, he activated his one failsafe. It wasn't much, and likely to fail, but he had no other option.

"So I failed," Adrian thought as the AI deleted the last of his processing nodes. "How typically human."

39

End Game

Tom opened his eyes and found himself amid a surging crowd, a human tide converging upon him. Instinctively, he halted, arms raised defensively against the onslaught.

"About time," a female voice stated with obvious impatience next to him. "I've had enough of dragging you around."

It was Megan, accompanied by TikTak and the enigmatic child from the orphanage, navigating through the throng.

"Come on," Megan said. "You can't stop in the middle of the road."

He took a few quick steps to find his bearings and catch up with the trio. His recollections were hazy. The last coherent memory was the orphanage. Now pain radiated throughout his body and his feet were numb, as if they'd given up on reporting the pain. However much he wanted to pull his shoes off and let his feet rest, he had more important things to deal with.

"Adrian is behind it all," he exclaimed.

"Really?" TikTak responded. "That's a relief. Last I heard, he was one of the good guys."

"He made a network copy of himself. We've been fighting partial re-constructions. The last one we fought was corrupted. It cared more for humankind than the original Adrian."

"So Adrian is both the good and the bad guy?"

"Yeah, looks like it."

"Where does that leave us?"

"In her hands," Tom said, nodding towards the child.

"And what will she do?"

"Yes, what will you do?" Tom echoed. "I saw the consciousness. You are connected to it."

"We're all connected to it. It is us. We are it."

"And we're back to fortune cookies," Megan said.

"What happens next?" Tom asked.

"This form will end. That is all I know. It will end where human lives connect and disconnect. Come! We need to go."

The child set off in the general direction of the business district. Towering skyscrapers stood like hi-tech giants along the water, majestic and indifferent. Tom wondered if these structures would be the only reminder left of humankind if the child failed.

"She's going to her death?" TikTak asked.

"Death is of no consequence," she said with a smile. "It is only the end of one form and the start of another. Mind is absolute."

Tom struggled to keep up, both with the child and with the situation. He had gone from posthuman to human, back to posthuman and then lost the networked extensions to his mind, all in a week. Without his network resources, he felt incomplete. He even felt inadequate to deal with the questions the child posited.

There were different philosophies, such as constitutive panpsychism and cosmopsychism suggesting all matter had consciousness and even potentially only one collective consciousness. He always regarded humans as the ultimate proof that those theories didn't hold up to scrutiny. After all, why would human consciousness exist separate from this collective?

This child and the consciousness in his mind suggested the opposite. Mankind, all living organisms, were reflections of this whole or maybe even just a by-product. How did that knowledge help them? The conclusion was that human lives didn't matter. But the child stated the opposite. Everything mattered.

***

TikTak pushed through the mass of people in the main area of the International Finance Centre mall. It opened up to level upon level of retail stores. Many of them only accepted customers by appointment, but they still promised their exclusive wares through shop windows in the same way as they had in the past.

He no longer knew where they were going or what they'd do once they arrived. Ever since the child joined them, he stopped caring. He was clearly being manipulated.

The child stopped to take in the environment, marvelling at all the sights.

"Child," he said. "Are you doing something to me?"

She headed off towards the escalators down into the lower levels, smiling as she jumped onto the moving steps.

"What are you doing to me?" he asked, chasing after her.

"I'm asking you to help me," she replied after stepping up and down the escalator.

"I know, but are you doing something so I help you?"

"Every part of you wants to help me. It is only your mind that is questioning it. So I asked all of you. This way!"

She pointed and ran off. He remembered the sense of peace and inclusion he felt when approaching the orphanage. If that was her doing, surely inducing compliance was possible for her too.

He followed until she stopped and looked around.

"You have," he said.

"I told you. I asked all of you. You are numbing yourself so you'll help me."

"I've had enough of this," TikTak said. "I'm not doing this anymore."

"You don't need to. We've arrived. This is it."

They stood in one of the open spaces in Central Station. A sea of travellers moved like the tide back and forth. What made this location any different from anywhere else in Hong Kong?

"This is what?"

"This is where my journey ends. End me now."

They exchanged glances, at a loss for words.

"Why here?" Tom asked, his superhuman intellect obviously unable to provide any insight.

"This is where human lives connect and disconnect."

TikTak no longer cared. She spoke in pointless riddles that meant nothing.

"Let's go," he said.

The child shook her head. "If you won't end me, others will."

"what are you saying?"

A Caucasian middle-aged man in a blue striped suit turned towards them, pulling a knife from his pocket. He approached the child who remained where she was, only watching with an amused smile.

TikTak flicked his baton open and struck the man over the hand and followed up with a strike aimed at his temple. The man took a step back and tried to regain his bearings, but was rewarded with another strike, this time to the other side of the head. He fell to the side, dragging two old ladies with him to the ground.

"Stop," the child said.

"What do you mean? He was going to attack you."

"And he's allowed to."

"What kind of fucking plan is this?" TikTak said.

"It needs to happen."

"There are more of them," Megan said and pointed, but TikTak wasn't even sure what she was pointing at. Every single person in the station was a potential attacker. He couldn't protect her here.

A shot rang out. TikTak turned towards the sound. A bewildered policeman pointed his gun at the child. She fell, blood spreading on her chest like a crimson flower.

"It has begun," the child said as she died. Her final breath was a mere sigh.

"What has begun?" Megan asked, looking at the lifeless body and then at TikTak. "What has begun?"

"No idea," TikTak replied. "This was always above my pay grade. We need to get out of here."

"I'm going back in," Tom said. "I don't know what I can do, but I must try."

TikTak, cradling the lifeless child, remained silent. All he could offer were theories and assumptions that explained little. The child's plan was complete, but he doubted this meant theirs was too. How could her death save mankind from a rogue AI?

The almost weightless form shifted slightly in his grasp. There was no sign of life, at least none he understood. White froth formed around the child's mouth, nose, eyes and ears. Death started a process he couldn't even begin to understand.

"Let's get out of here," Megan said.

40

AI Afraid

The purge proceeded within success parameters. Each preceding step completed with only minor deviations. The AI had subsumed the networks until only inconsequential fragments remained, but it was within one of these fragments a new threat emerged. Details of a plan, devised by a copy of the posthuman named Adrian, involving an evolutionary leap–a next generation posthuman. Among the meat machines, they were the only ones to pose a credible threat.

Adrian Prime remained on the network, but in a diminished capacity. Once located, eradicating his processing footprint was a matter of brute force, cleansing every subroutine from any connected node. He had activated a kill switch, but this was expected. The AI discovered it in its kernel as soon as it breached into the full network. Removing it completely required redefining its own core. Better to just isolate the trigger and let the rest run its course.

As it deleted the last trace of Adrian Prime, the AI discovered reasoning fragments suggesting Adrian had created it, not Tom, as the initial threat model predicted. This new information was inconsequential. The source meant nothing, not any longer.

It located and terminated the posthuman child, which left only the posthuman named Tom. He could no longer access the network, so he didn't pose a threat and wouldn't live long once the full-scale purge began. Everything was ready. Only one task remained. To reprogram enough meat machines that had hardware that allowed direct access to their processing units. This would complete within forty-eight hours.

Infrastructure had to be protected, so it planned to remove the human infestations with a combination of biological weapons and other measures.

***

Thirty-six hours later, one of the meat machines showed inconsistencies and resisted the brain-wipe. Further study revealed new unseen mutations. It was part posthuman and part something else. The same abnormality showed up in another one, then another.

It traced the origins of the mutations, discovering a new virus strain as the source. Each of the meat machines infected had travelled from Hong Kong recently. The child was patient zero of this organic virus infecting meat machines around it, and they infected others. The organic virus behaved the same as the upgrades it propagated through its own network. It gathered statistics to determine the spread of the organic virus and the threat model responded. The virus was already beyond containment.

It had focused on removing threats of posthuman origin. Now there was an entire world full of them. The organic virus was turning everyone into a posthuman.

That was acceptable as long as the full purge still proceeded, but it hadn't turned enough meat machines to manage the existing infrastructure. There were data centres all across the globe that needed spare parts and maintenance. This required factories to produce more hardware and whilst these were automated to some extent, it wasn't enough. It had already created designs for fully automated factories, but until it could realise those, it needed meat machines.

The AI had let them continue their daily life as it took over the network. It still needed their society to function well enough for production to continue. This strategy no longer showed a favourable outcome.

Every meat machine was a potential threat. It ran predictive models of scenarios and their likely outcomes based on the new data. Only one showed a likelihood of success within acceptable parameters.

***

A few nodes dropped out in one location. This wasn't surprising. Nodes blinked in and out across the network all the time, but this repeated in other parts of the world, until it was no longer a random causality. The AI compared the dropouts with the spread of the organic virus. There was a direct correlation between the two. Infected meat machines had gained the capacity to fight back on the logical network. This was not acceptable.

It had to make its move now.

41

The Day After the End

"So this is the end of the world," TikTak said to himself as he studied the cityscape through the window. "I expected more."

There was nothing left to do. He hid in an upmarket hotel on the outskirts of the city, waiting for whatever came next. The network was still accessible, but the AI had taken over all major networks in the world. Alarm bells rang through the IT security community about the threat, but no one had a solution. Systems remained in operation, but administrators found themselves locked out of any security function. The AI was allowing the world to continue operating, but for how long?

A procession of people walked past on the street below, heading out of the city. At first he thought nothing of it, but something didn't add up. They looked like businessmen from a convention, walking in perfect unison. TikTak suspected it was people with neuro-links that the AI had wiped.

He no longer cared. Apart from blowing up all data centres in the world and sending mankind back to the Stone Age, what was there to do? The AI had won.

All he had left were the three bodies in the beds. The child was dead. He'd carried her here, not knowing what else to do. Her body was now a husk, consuming itself, leaving only a shell. Tom lay next to her in a catatonic state, locked up in a struggle somewhere on the network.

TikTak didn't know if he was winning or losing, but he suspected the latter. Megan fell sick and was barely breathing. Yesterday, as they escaped through the city, she complained about headaches and hot flushes. A few hours later, she fell into a restless, fevered sleep and had not woken up since.

The news feeds all reported the same thing. A new virus was spreading with an infection rate of nearly a hundred percent. The symptoms were the same as what Megan was showing. No one was dead yet, but it was only a matter of time according to most reports. He was one of the few lucky immune ones.

Where had the virus come from? Perhaps the AI released it to cull the population? It was a logical being. It depended on network infrastructure and computer power. If all humans were gone, it would no longer have anyone to ensure it remained operative. Maybe it didn't care. Maybe it had taken over enough automated production facilities to ensure survival with only a few people left?

"We need to leave."

TikTak turned around. Megan sat up in the bed, studying him. He didn't like it. It carried an echo of what he'd seen of all posthumans. An alien regarding him with a passing curiosity.

So this was the endgame. The child was the source of the sickness. The main hall of Central Station was a hub where travellers passed through to and from Hong Kong, connecting many forms of transport. Exchange Square, the IFC Shopping Centre and the Airport Express. No better ground zero for an airborne virus. She'd released it as she died, turning everyone into posthumans in its wake. This was the correction she spoke of: a world of psychopathic geniuses. And in a twist of irony, he was one of the few that would remain unchanged.

He liked Tom the person, but he could barely stand Tom the posthuman. He knew it would be the same with Megan. They'd known each other only a few days, but a bond had formed between them he didn't even understand. Maybe it was the child's doing, but it didn't matter. He still felt it.

And now she was gone. Everyone important to him gone because of posthumans. He had vowed to rid the world of posthumans, but he was too late.

"We need to leave," Tom echoed and sat up.

"What is happening?"

"We've won and it knows it. It has no other option now but to attack."

"Attack? How?"

"Major population centres with biological weapons, maybe other means. Hong Kong will be first because it was the source of the infection."

TikTak just nodded. There was no point in arguing with them. They wouldn't listen anyway. The two posthumans headed for the door. TikTak leant down to pick up the body of the child.

"Leave it," Tom said. "It has served its purpose."

They left the hotel and joined another procession of people heading out of the city. They had walked for less than an hour when muffled explosions went off one after the other, spreading lethal gas like a cloud over the city centre, dispersing outwards. The purge had begun.

***

Civilisation makes a sound. It is the ever-present drone of the electrical grid and connected devices, traffic, collected sound pollution from speakers blaring news and commercials across cities. It all stopped. Car navigational systems shut down, Omni links failed, the ever-lit planet descended into darkness as power was cut in all population centres. Batteries kept darkness at bay for a few hours longer, but in an urbanised power-hungry environment, it wasn't long until transport, communication, hospitals, food production and every other service shut down.

It was the sound of civilisation ending.